Young L'adorsity

DS Swanson

ISBN 978-1-387-43658-3

The Great United Territories
of America
at the
Dawning of the Third Millenium

Note: The following narrative is composed entirely in the Immigrant Tongue, a dialect which may be unfamiliar to some. However, with small effort, these words shall be decipherable by any reasoning being—possibly even, with considerably more effort, by the British.

Invitation

Have you chanced wonder, Dear Reader, which lonely soul shall seek within pages stark and dry that Gift even life's experience troubles not to bring?

All have, one hopes, for hope breathes innate in the trying—faith fervent against counsel of the real, that what transpires within may ring real enough, even be it formed solely of imagination, color, life and glory that ne'er may another perceive. 'tween story and reader emerges bond most verdant, living two as one—union in a yarn, inspiration of mere diversion. Is here not truth of a sort, spark of no words from words, believed before understood? These arrive as intuitions pure; beckons the promise...

Therefore draw near. Cast walls of doubt low and let the beautiful child believe. Dear Reader, this is our story, a telling unique as breathed of you.

Orson

Much is to be explained as to places and times, but a placid start feels right. Defer the histories and imagine, simply, night.

Warm night, and in the humid airs swim mighty scents, of nearby pastures and ripening fields.

Dark, not opaque; dim pastels bloom, grassy greens washed gray and blue by waxing moon. A wide, easy meadow opens in shallow waves, flanked at a distance by crouching trees, silhouettes black before seraph-sprinkled heavens eons away. Oh, stars! Brilliant wash of them forms an arc over quiescent lands below.

Meadow and sky are one, and in the meadow sits one man.

Having created him, we cannot ignore him. Questions form—why shall a lone spirit inhabit a meadow by night? Rather than guess, simply let us descend mid-moment upon him in that clandestine way stories do, to learn what we may learn.

Not much to see at first, just a stranger: young, blond, rugged clothes not the cleanest. He wears riding boots and sits cross-legged—no easy feat—and a worn leather hat rests within arm's reach upon the grass. Silent is he, revealing little as to what his character may contain. Is he hero or foe? Will fondness grow as he speaks and acts, or perhaps distaste?

But wait, this is special; no speech and no action. Just a man sitting—and the night knows not of the many nights that have come before, and so tries with eager zeal to Be. He allows it, and so it Is: a violent force of splendor in an understated twinkle of mind's eye—missed easily were not pure motive on hand to focus conscious light upon it. Some have felt a mighty presence of self in such times, of nothing and everything one. A calm exhale, aware, and behold! The night soaks straight through and is still. The cricket chirps and distant planetary sounds are the world calling out, "Listen…"

Here is one style of being, of peace which settles spontaneous within.

We know there are others—those who would know pain of chaos in these same times, cyclones of conflict swirling mindless within mind, desires deaf and blind. For these the good of the senses merely shall be sensing the dull, as the boring inevitably grow bored and boorishly bore themselves further— especially having brought no liquor. Such a bother, clarity.

We know these, for we take their side often enough. A moment a moment is, wrong and then right; and if we find moments right, later we will not—no method exists as to their perfection.

But pure motive—said before—always serves as able sharpener of the senses, to the wonderful things.

Therefore we learn something already, of a solitary man

and of nights and peace. Admiration for this nameless character surely grows, if motive be the sole power he holds to exist in all stillness, feeling not unwelcome by the cosmos itself.

The present moment passes away, as promised, prey to the coming of a second nameless stranger.

The sound of him sneaks into existence from crickets' din, beneath awareness' brink for a time, later emerging fully formed. As noises go, we must agree it is peculiar for these surroundings. A rhythmic click and whir punctuate a continuous husky grind, as a soft wheel upon gravel.

Two wheels, to be precise.

It grows up from the direction of the township, where a dirt road marches 'tween many a field of sugar-beet and sunflower. As well, a spark of light is born, appearing and disappearing, source eclipsed at times by stalks or stands of trees. Such patient disturbance it is, increasing in measured increment, that soon it feels as though the earlier busy silences never were.

Click and watery swish—the wheels leave the road and enter the grass of the meadow, close now. And the man sitting can dimly see the source of the commotion: a bicycle mated with a torch, bouncing along, each jolt sending the harried flame blowing downward and upward.

The new visitor is off-beam by a considerable margin, looking to be aimed for the neighboring field. The contraption barely misses a gathering of drowsy cattle, then lurches to a stop, the torch sending a shower of sparks futile against damp earth.

A tall figure dismounts.

"Skeeter! Skeeter L'adorsity, have you arrived?" Still is the voice, muted by distance and humid air. Less helpful, the visitor is facing the wrong direction.

The calm one rises almost regretfully; for the start of this means the true end of the last. His movements are graceful: up

3

from the cross-legged position by one leg and no hands—a twist, then the other leg down to stand straight. The combination leaves him facing toward the visitor.

"Here, 'tis he," Skeeter L'adorsity calls with a voice sure for his common size.

Now the name of our character is known, and we have heard him speak. As for the other, let us spoil some mysteries before they grow tiresome. He is familiar to Skeeter, being acquainted nearly from birth: best friend, adversary, and, as years pass, best friend again—never admitting to having been otherwise. Where one chooses left, the other surely chooses right. For one a flighty manner, the other a modest, near-painfully measured countenance. One pragmatic in deceit, the other unaccountably candid to his gentle core. Two men, each to balance and confine the other's foible. Roles within roles they play, switching oft as a pair of sparring puppies, madly rolling and biting and never seeming to find injury.

Tonight the other, let us call him Orson, wishes he were the wiser—but sadly, his best navigation has placed him in the wrong field. Even so, meadows appear alike in the dark; thus he attempts a grand bluff.

The glowing torch comes free from the bicycle's basket with a tug. Orson turns to wander a crooked pattern toward Skeeter's voice, calling out, "My friend, why are your bearings so poor? A family trait, no doubt. Was not Father L'adorsity always misguided as well, and Mother too? I reel in surprise, that they found one another in order to conceive you..."

The calm one inclines to refuse bait so obvious. He bends to collect his hat from the grass, sets it atop his head and begins at a measured pace toward a patch of meadow across which the other will pass—provided the course does not change at random, as happens with Orson.

The other continues the taunt, squinting into the dark

beyond his upheld torch. "How will dear Jonathan find us in these fields when you lead us so far astray?"

Skeeter feels an uncharacteristic flush as this new fact extracts itself from the muddle: 'twas Jonathan who set the meeting! The message Orson left before was cryptic, mentioning only time and place—and no circumstance. With trepidation does Skeeter accept any such invitation; yet, for all the wisdom his youthful soul possesses, he thinks never of refusing.

Naïveté, a tragic flaw.

Jonathan Turner: another companion nearly from birth, but not a friend in any way, save familiarity and necessity. A sinister presence lives upon that one, such that a single glance loudly does scream every clouded secret. Skeeter assumes every man can sense what he knows, even trusts others as fellow watchers over the Dark One. But mistaken is he; only young L'adorsity has the power of discerning these things.

Orson, tired of taunting, takes to good natured teasing. "Come you my way, sir, or shall I return to the township to rally a search for your half-eaten remains?"

Skeeter's voice booms at last, close enough to cause his friend a start. "Who shall stalk me, these fierce cattle?" A nearby cow moos to punctuate the comment, and he allows a smile for sweet coincidence.

"Cows have been known to attack, should a man be foolish to corner one. Perhaps the monotony of the grassy diet drives them to kill…"

"Why shall any creature kill, with a full belly?"

The two have now located one another, partway up a gentle rise in the meadow. Orson—pale skinned, dark haired, lanky as lanky ever could be—holds the higher ground, peering down further than he is accustomed. And Skeeter, the shorter, troubles not to face upward.

Instead he regards a single misplaced daisy, white petals

5

lavender in the gloom, its home now perilously near to Orson's soiled boot. The fidgety foot bounces to and fro, threatening to crush the flower at any moment.

But while his body is ever active, Orson's mouth is suddenly and uncharacteristically still. Momentary purpose achieved, he waits, discretely scanning the dark horizon for the coming of the next visitor…

Skeeter reluctantly sheds his detachment and speaks—for he possesses no clue as to the nature of this evening's plans.

"Orson, trusted friend. Your message earlier found me in best of spirits; I'd been about the field lands, receiving the last of the sunset. I came here straightaway, and my peace held true all the while darkness has gathered. But now, with your arrival, my hopeful spirit is fled. You bring trouble." Thoughts shared, Skeeter returns to the drama of the daisy, watching with just keener interest.

Meanwhile Orson feigns surprise. "You say you came here straightaway? I gave your mother the message to meet when the moon was high."

"Indeed, she relayed your intent with clarity. 'twas my choice to arrive early."

"Goodness, why?"

"I enjoy the likes of this place, solitude's sweet caress upon my ear."

"Solitude's sweet caress? A strange one is what they say of you." The tall one snorts polite disgust, still moving in small circles frenetic as his thoughts. Thankfully he orbits away from the defenseless flower.

"Very well," Skeeter sighs, to dismiss the point.

But Orson is intent, grinning meanly. "Are you certain the cattle of these fields are safe from your ill designs? By sweet solitude caress you more than their ears?"

Skeeter, silent, finds no humor in such offense.

"Never you mind, young soul," Orson continues. "A joke is all. To think we are both of twenty-two years; born days apart. And how could any be less worldly than young L'adorsity?" Then, at last appraising Skeeter's dark stare, he relents to the issue at hand. "I bring no trouble, friend. Only opportunity. A business meeting we shall have."

"A business meeting…in a meadow? Does not home or tavern beckon reasonable men?"

"But for the lucrative nature of the work being offered, I would have so chosen."

"Characters involved cry malice."

"Jonathan…" Orson says, absently, conceding his earlier slip of the tongue.

"He is coming, I surmise. A fact you omitted in your invitation."

"An oversight. I'd forgotten…you two, and your minor feud." Orson stops, sighs, hand on hip, his body a passive telling of displeasure. "Still, I believe we shall hear a fair offer from him—only a fool declines an offer not heard."

Skeeter finds small amusement in the other's irritation. "Perhaps I shall escape this dark cloud—is a lie not that?—and leave you two to your meeting."

"You would leave now? My timid friend, I hide nothing," the tall one protests, waving the flaming torch distractedly. "I know little as you of this business." He resumes wandering with blundering steps, one boot at last crushing the frail stem of the daisy. The brave soldier falls without a cry, petals intact but lacking future. Skeeter winces. Orson, oblivious of revenge taken, brings himself near. "I pray you, linger a time further. Jonathan will be arriving. Let him enlighten, that we weigh his offer charily before accepting."

Skeeter sighs and turns away. He scans the field of unseen things for the man of unseen things to come. Orson falls silent as well, aware of somehow having won the exchange. He adjusts the hat on his head, fidgets with the tassel.

Then he lowers his voice for no good reason, and at last reveals a bit of what he is hiding: "'tis time you learned how men live, old friend…"

Skeeter turns back. "How men live?"

"I have implored Jonathan to include you in our business, that you at last become one."

"That I become…"

"A man."

Orson chuckles, lightness returned. Skeeter stares again, with ice, the subject being one of old and uneasy familiarity.

"You call me less the man. What shall be the reason today?"

"The same as every day…for that everlasting innocence you wear about you like a little girl's frilly dress. People see you coming and say: 'Look, 'tis young L'adorsity the simple, Young L'adorsity the stunted runt-child.' My heart is with you, for I know the truth: that short of life you are—never having tasted life's sweet fulfillments."

"Are not life's sweetest fulfillments of the tranquil sort?"

"Save tranquility for old age, young stallion. Where is your thirst for wine, lust for women? Love is ever afoot, awaiting your slightest glance…and for naught. I am disturbed of watching it, your life's passing, the upper school years, the girls of University."

"University…who scored highest there?"

"You did, of course—to little gain. We shall settle and find work in farm and factory, where talk of schoolwork and grades is long forgot by bitter men. This, our future, is upon us— shall we forsake fond memories as well?"

Orson's enthusiasm never ebbs when fulfillments and panaceas are under discussion. He reeks of both this very moment, clear being his activities prior to coming here.

"Life is good," Skeeter at last glowers. "The land prospers—still you devise much upon which to fret. You trouble two minds this eve with your discontent. 'tis a sickness I fear contracting; already I feel ill…"

The tone is effective, if not the words—for he has allowed his voice to find an uncharacteristic timbre, as of a spiteful father. The night has changed color. Orson yields, turns and sees the flower lying stricken. He scoops it and stuffs it into the band of his hat, an impromptu accessory.

The end of conversation has birthed a silence, wherein a small sound already dwells—the clip-clop of shoed horse hooves.

The next visitor approaches, and the darkness transforms still further.

Jonathan

A little girl plays in a sandbox, painted wooden doll in hand, singing. Five years old, hair perfect straight, eyes powder blue—and she is full of the moment.

Her child voice sings, and a young boy listens nearby, sharing in its perfection. Life is grand in this wildish yard, of grasses and rocks beneath a great sticky tree.

Savage! A big boy like a shadow appears and snatches the doll, holding it high, laughing, taunting. No singing now, only the sad sound of her wailing. The boy listening rises gracefully. Life becomes rage in this wildish yard.

A stone arcs with uncanny aim. It strikes the big boy at the temple. He howls and runs, and the doll bounces to the ground. The girl-child has her doll again, but there is no more singing.

Thunderous hooves turn to muted thumps as the horse enters the meadow, approaching from the township along the same route Orson followed before. Finding is easy with the light of the torch betraying their position.

Jonathan is upon them, menacing and tall atop a glistening black horse.

The animal, his prize mare, is frisky from the ride; she rocks surly at her master holding her still with taut rein. Jonathan comes clad in the same manner as Orson and Skeeter, but his clothing is of finer make. Over his hat, a thin gauze masks his face against the mosquitoes that swarm these parts—to which he has always been most susceptible. His hair, by day the color of stained walnut, shows dark orange by the light of the torch, his long face the color of flame. That face now turns from side to side behind the netting, eyeing one man then the other.

"This one," he says sullenly. "Why is he here?" The question is to Orson regarding Skeeter—a patently rude beginning—and Skeeter realizes that Jonathan had no foreknowledge of his coming. Orson's orchestrations are far-reaching indeed.

Ignoring this, and having little risk of the moment becoming worse, Skeeter decides to address the man on the horse with strong initiative. "Perhaps the query for which you search is: why has young L'adorsity honored you with his presence, having undertaken all effort to be here at such inopportune place and hour?"

Jonathan opens his mouth for an ill-tempered response, then stops. His head tips back and he laughs loudly. Orson follows suit, and more loudly, trying mightily to ease the tension so sudden and strong. Skeeter simply waits, aware that if all three laugh it be for entirely disparate reasons.

"Come down here," Orson urges, "and let us reason together. I have much in mind for these enterprises of yours,

11

Dear Jonathan; some of my thoughts include our friend Skeeter."

Jonathan considers his next move briefly, then complies with a smooth dismount, ending the standoff. The mare wanders off a few yards. She tries to graze, troubled by the bit that has not been loosed. Jonathan ignores the animal and turns to the men. When he speaks, his voice has a sing-song quality, as if every word were rehearsed. "Very well. As long history does unite us in this township, let old animosities fall aside, that there be proper discussion among men."

"Hear, hear," says Orson, as though a toast has been made.

"I am told of a job offer," Skeeter says, wearying of inane banter. "What sort of work is it?"

Jonathan looks to Orson. "He does not know?"

"For discretion's sake, I thought it best that you reveal the details," Orson explains. The two chuckle; for Jonathan now realizes the game, it being at Skeeter's expense.

The torch sputters and dies at that moment, blind of dark overcoming all 'till eyes can adjust.

Skeeter struggles to see the others. "What? What is the job?"

"Orson and you are to be messengers, simple as that."

"What sort of messengers? Regarding illicit matters?" The harebrained question hangs in the air, pointless for the obviousness of its answer. "Illicit matters, of course," Skeeter adds, as correction.

"You know I am a man of business in the township," Jonathan explains, "with many a venture here and there, near and far…high and low. 'tis of the low business we speak this eve."

Skeeter waits, checks the moon and wonders about the time. Were it not for the first part of the evening, that spent in solitude, this would be an outing most pointless.

Orson, ever impatient, picks up where the other has

paused. "What Jonathan is telling us, old friend, is that we shall not be required to engage in any unlawful acts ourselves. We shall simply...deliver information regarding other...items, none of which we need involve ourselves with directly. Unless we...choose to be involved. Directly."

At the last phrase, both men share another chuckle.

"I for one rather enjoy being...involved," Jonathan adds, "when discretion allows."

"I accept your offer, Jonathan," Orson says. Then he addresses Skeeter. "And what of you? Accept you our old friend's generous proposition?"

"Despite your best efforts, I remain unaware of the nature of this work," Skeeter answers, vexation finally edging his voice.

The chuckling continues, but finally Orson relents. "Prostitutes!"

"Messengers...for prostitutes?"

"Indeed, couriers and nothing more. You fetch one of Jonathan's ladies, that you may inform her of her next...business meeting. You need but a mind, a memory for figures."

"You need a horse," Jonathan adds. "Or a bicycle."

"As you know, I have no bicycle, and my family keeps no horses."

"You may use mine." Orson motions toward where he believes his bicycle stands on the next hill—bearing skewed, of course.

"And the pay?"

Orson looks to Jonathan to answer, the question being the only matter of which he did not possess full knowledge the entire time.

Jonathan is silent, pretending to mull figures. Finally he says, "I can spare...a dollar an hour, a dollar and half if profits are good. You may also take your pay in...favors."

"Very well," Skeeter answers calmly. "When shall we

13

begin?"

Orson and, to a lesser measure, Jonathan stare open-mouthed at the reply.

The incredulity subsides and Jonathan continues. "It seems where I sought one, I have found two. A shared vocation it will be, of course, for I need but one at a spell. Argue between you over who reports and who rests. Begin tomorrow, noon, East Moorhead Park. I shall give you instructions at that time, your pay by day's end." He turns to find his horse.

Orson, beaming, leans close to Skeeter. "Fine choice," he whispers. "But why have you relented so easily in this matter? With you, impropriety provokes resistance, always ..."

"To agree is best to end a dull conversation; a dollar a fair wage." Skeeter leaves silent his last motive.

Jonathan, again on horseback, jogs the beast sideward to tower over them. "Let us make a contract then." He extends an arm down and they grasp in a three-way handshake. "Date it thus, May 2, 2001. Three gentlemen have made arrangement; let all follow in good faith, and let it be so bound."

"Let it be so bound," the others repeat as one, in the standard form of verbal agreement.

At the touch of Jonathan's hand, Skeeter shrinks within, for all good and evil may be inferred by the warm or cold of a man's skin. What horrors live there—lies, rape...murder? If not past, then future; 'tis difficult to divine particulars.

To associate with such a being is to perturb the conscience. More troubling is young L'adorsity's empathy toward the other's proud flavor of shame. It attacks the better man as a weighty sadness, leaving him sick at his stomach.

He pulls away quickly as the handshake is finished.

Business complete, Jonathan is gone, the mare at a lope along the road back to Moorhead.

As for the remaining two, all conversation is exhausted

before, tempers stretched. None but polite good-eves beg saying.
Orson manages to locate his bicycle in the dark and speeds off,
presumably late for an important social gathering.

Young L'adorsity begins the long walk home, his chosen
companion, the good night, returning to comfort him. He
breathes clear air, that recent stenches be washed away.

Prostitutes…in Moorhead? Such truths must exist, he
supposes, yet ne'er has he shown them attention. Even now he
accepts only the abstract, remaining aloof from bleak details—
which surely shall intrude at a point.

At the least, these events as have occurred are strange;
perhaps an elemental departure has occurred. He is confident,
however.

For young L'adorsity, that which is not sleep is
amusement; and the world remains, overall, a safe place.

Batiste

Morning! Dawn like day, springtime sky ablaze. Moorhead, crown of the Dakotas, rouses spry. Citizens prepare a full day of love and conquest. Beneath proud buildings, some probing high as twelve layers, streets commence to fill with horses, automobiles and bicycles in equal measure.

This is modern by any appraisal, the most advanced in any of the United Territories. Nearly all here have plumbing and disposal; and the fingers of an electric grid creep further year by year, to power new machines in the day, a galaxy of incandescent bulbs by night.

'tis a learned culture as well, the matter having been agreed by vote—that education be free and compulsory through four years of University. Such sophistication keeps ever alive the love of eloquent language and scruple, and good people find endless means for its integration into their ways of life.

Eloquence shall be the norm, so long as we visit this world.

And what of this world of 2012? What of these great United Territories of America, stretching from the Atlantic nearly to the Rockies?

Dear Reader, perhaps now is an apt time to reveal that this world may be different from the world you know. Ever so dull is the habit of placing all tales in the same universe, even while myriad possibilities pique imagination. Many histories can exist, and do, each unique in all its subtle beauties. From what other place shall our stories spring, but a multi-verse which spins them real?

Therefore let the setting for our story be a time of good seasons—in particular, a world of changes as may be conceived by a succession thereof. Imagine long history born of brimming harvests, steady provision, none affected by drought or fiscal distraction. Picture a world of peaceful commerce, untested by atrocity of war. A race of innocents may this engender, perhaps, compared with the lot born of less lucky worlds?

So rare is conflict between nations that even the independence of The United Territories was achieved by merely an ugly argument. No musket shot split the sky. Not a man lost his life. Now slaves live free, natives and immigrants work as brothers, and men till the land to the profit of all.

These prosperities surely prove the innate goodness of human creatures, if well-fed men have so little incentive toward war. Perhaps.

Or perhaps a few good seasons expend themselves to naught. Perhaps hard times bear little blame for crimes transpired. Human want stirring as it may, more than comforts shall we crave. Dark passions linger and consume, even in the gentlest weather.

Now you have your histories, Dear Reader, and let us

delay further musings, for, look! Our character is awake, stirring with the morning's first sunbeam across his face.

The room in which he sleeps looks east, and in the spring he keeps merely a sheer fabric for a window. The air sways brisk; last night's crickets are transformed to birds.

The L'adorsity home—at the west end of the township and beyond the Red River—is a place of basic comfort, more a beneficiary to external progress than greatness from within. A respectable plot of land with space enough for goats and chickens and a garden in the rear, a high-steeped house washed pure white, and only four reside there—for the family survives a lost son. Aside from young L'adorsity, there remain only Mother and Father and Mother's Mother.

Father has run off to work, even in this early hour, and so there are three. Grandmother is…old and unaware, and so there are two. Mother is asleep, and so there is one…solitude.

Each day begins with a breath, consciousness, where follows the first intention of the morning. Skeeter L'adorsity delays the latter, remaining cozy, waiting for the day to seduce him. Sleepily he rolls to his feet.

Still without intention, he acts by habit, first to check the health of Grandmother in the next bedroom. The old woman breathes; no funeral today. He moves about the room noisily, tidying, removing soiled towels, unconcerned with waking the deaf. She snores ugly songs all the while, to which he listens— ever amused by the sheer perfection of disharmony.

What a woman she once was! When her mind was sound her doting presence warmed the house. But now—perhaps the family's loss has accelerated her loss—she is without speech, absent emotion or reaction to words and touch.

Still, the good grandson remains true, pending the finish of the matter; he perseveres in love, inspired by memories of better days.

When he has finished with Grandmother, he passes through the drawing room, where black-and-white family photographs hang grainy over the rarely-touched liquor cabinet. In one, a man of twenty-two and a boy of twelve smile diligently for the long camera exposure—Batiste L'adorsity, firstborn son, and his child brother. Skeeter's eyes avoid the faces, the eldest of which has become nearly his twin—he was once the younger boy. Ten years it has taken to replace Batiste, in appearance, if not in talent or personality.

Beyond the kitchen is the water closet, installed a few years previous. He washes himself, still charmed by the novelty of indoor plumbing.

Disappointments follow. First, he recalls the events of last eve—the job he took to spite a friend's expectation. The best was that brief satisfaction; today the commitment must be honored, and little joy springs from the thought. Still, dismay survives but a moment, as a schedule commences forming in his mind. It will be a day of visits then: first a stop at Father's office, as is customary, then Orson's house; for in their haste they neglected the decision of who will report to Jonathan today and who will rest. Should it come to pass—and he believes it will—the next visit shall be to Jonathan, dark cloud and all, at high noon in an adjacent borough of Moorhead.

Following that visit, the day is blank; he has no imagination as to what strange—and perchance disturbing—visits the job may require.

A second, albeit minor, disappointment comes as he tends to the animals of the back yard, their braying and clucking love of him and his bag of feed piercing the easy morning. Mother awakens, and his solitude is betrayed.

"Peter, dear," she calls, thin lips begetting the name she gave him twenty-two years ago. The way she utters it, she reclaims him to her, time and again. She is paused at the rear door of the house, gray in the shade 'neath brightening day, simple woman with not much to say.

"Always so early," she notes. "Like your father."

"Not so early that I shall ever win good Mr. L'adorsity," Skeeter replies as he stows the feed and enters the kitchen, scraping dark mud from his boots. "I am up with the dawn and still…he is working."

"Your father is of the dedicated species; more god than man, oftentimes."

Young L'adorsity concedes her point with a brief grin. "I fail him, being merely human."

Mother enjoys jokes less than most, and so subjects shift often, of necessity. "Breakfast," she concludes.

"Good." He smiles appeasement. "No demigod ought starve."

Breakfast comes into being of smells, crackling grease and utensil sounds. Mother and son eat in silence, fortunately a preference in common, and afterward he enjoys cleaning the kitchen. Mother packs a portion of the breakfast into the old picnic basket, hands it to him and says: "For Father…"

With a nod, the good son takes the basket, finds his hat and leaves his home…over green of yard, gray of road, through a neighborhood still deserted. The day is begun.

Father's office waits on a main avenue, a few blocks south. Skeeter walks, eyes closed for a time, smelling jasmine and black walnut. Tepid air swims heavy across his face. He opens his eyes, to squint in the bright. Last eve's glittered sky is now splashed with blunted arcs of blue-white. Along the streets, sun-painted trees prove belief in a thousand hues of green, each unique with garnish of yellow and gold. The volume of energy renders the day surreal—strange magic adds to form, as spirit to experience, each instant a world in itself.

Still half a block away from the office, he catches the distinct tang of his father's cigar smoke, as everything about the man occupies a grand radius of influence. When Skeeter enters the open doorway, he finds him lodged at the old angry desk, puffing and scribbling, surrounded by many a sheaf of paper and file. Large, stubby fingers of the right hand grasp the pen, while the left hand lies palm down upon the desk, formal against the depravity of idleness. Here is the father young L'adorsity sees all the moments of his life, even from the time he played amongst the legs of the same desk as a child.

A barrister by trade, determined man by character, yet Mr. L'adorsity manages to escape popularity in the township, even for his long years of dedicated service. As he has explained it many times 'round family dinners: farmers abide by farmers, businessmen by businessmen. None have love to spare for a wily lawyer, save one who holds key to escaping some legal predicament. When such troubles come, the people are warmth incarnate; while later, troubles eased, they withdraw to other worlds and the man is alone again.

Father takes no notice at the living son's entry, and the basket landing on the desk inspires only a grunt. Appreciation unspoken, love unshewn…all is atmospheric and implicit, affection a sort of faith ne'er concreted. 'tis sufficient to Skeeter's emaciated sensibilities, though. He turns to leave with no discontent.

"And what," comes the gruff voice, "today?"

Son stops and faces the desk. "You ask of my plans?"

Eyes are averted; thick gray eyebrows wiggle as Father writes, silent but for the scrape-scrape of the pen. Of course. University completed months previous, a son's inactivity is a puzzle to be solved. Father, of late, asks the same question every second day, always in a different guise.

"I have taken an occupation," Skeeter announces.

21

The pen stops, starts again. "This is good. Mother shall have no call to spoil you."

"Indeed. And I pay my keep, all the same; a man's code I shall live."

"Of what sort is the work?"

"The wage is a dollar and half." Skeeter glances away from Father, at the grand file drawers against the wall, wondering how much dust is collected at their lofty tops.

"Hmm. A fair wage. What is the work? Not...a grain refinery..."

"No. Of course, no."

Father is silent to indicate satisfaction.

"The time!" Skeeter says. "I am late, nearly so. Until this eve, Sir..." And he is a phantom, quickly out the door, content that Father will barely recall the exchange.

"Father has brought ice," says the older brother, "and Mother has been skimming cream all day..."

The younger brother stares with little understanding—but enjoying the anticipation in the other's voice.

Older brother laughs. "Silly Peter, you see nothing. Soon Mother will send us to market for sugar, and Father will start the mixing."

"Sugar!" exclaims the younger.

"No," corrects the older. "Ice cream!"

"Ice cream!"

The boys run to the kitchen, five-year-old outpacing fifteen-year-old. A block of ice perches majestic atop the hewn chopping block, but the room is oddly quiet. They turn to find Mother alone at the table, head leaned to the wall—dreaming at the air.

"Ice cream," the younger brother demands.

To which Mother smiles sadly, gathering herself back to

*the present. She faces her sons. "Ice cream, yes. Perhaps, if
Father returns in time…"*

*"Where has he gone now?" The older child's voice turns
sullen.*

*"Important business has arisen. Be patient and he will
return; of this I am sure…"*

*And so they remain at the table, the boys staring eagerly
at the ice block. By and by Mother wanders from the room to
attend to household duties. A pool of water forms beneath the
block, and later a gentle stream begins dripping, over
countertops and cabinets, searching for rest at the floor. 'tis an
intricate process, entertaining enough to watch for hours.*

*When the sun has sunk to dusk, the ice is barely a blob.
The older brother sighs and chides the younger. "Perhaps you
made Father angry, and for that he has forgotten us…"*

Violence…

*It comes quickly, ends, and leaves the fifteen-year-old
rubbing his bruised chin in surprise. The insult is rebuffed.*

*Young Peter, fist burning red, stares defiantly at Batiste
for a moment, then looks back to the ice.*

Thereafter, the two sit quietly.

Orson's house, the next stop. Nearby the river's edge he
resides, in a meager cottage with a mother and two sisters, a
father escaped and remarried in a distant township. As the
favored child, Orson warrants a private bedroom, with an
outsized window that opens to the front yard. One can enter this
way easily, so that Skeeter never can recollect having used the
front door.

The curtains are closed today, thick pleated fabric
blocking both light and polite entry. Skeeter raps the sill and,
after much time, a stirring comes from within. Orson's face
appears at the parted shades, eyes swollen with sleep.

There ensues an extended silence, narrated by songbirds up and down the street, as each waits for the other to speak.

Finally, Orson: "What is it, you fool?"

"Daytime, for one."

"Barely so."

"A special day, for another."

"Nothing is special today, save the sleep of which you deprive me."

"We have work. Hark back to your compelling proposal of just last eve"

"Yes, I know." Orson sighs. "Seek you test my resolve then? In that familiar manner ever do you mock me—with morning, my ungodly heel."

"Simply that the sun moves toward high noon, and we have decisions to effect."

"The sun is merciful slow, old friend. Time for rest we always have."

Orson, still holding the drapes together with awkward stance, shifts, and Skeeter catches glimpse into the dim room beyond. A girl sleeps nude, facing away, shadows painting her flesh in relief. 'tis beauty unforeseen, and Skeeter feels an uneasy lust stirring, envy for his friend's uncaring ways.

Then strikes a recollection, Orson's words of last eve, unwelcome lecture to a stunted runt-child. The stunted one now knows shame—not for his lust, but for his incapacity to act upon it, for the many facets of him that keep those living energies ever unripe.

He shrugs the feeling away, for by stubborn resolve can any man keep a moment magic; this is a powerful talent. But power can be sapped. A bitter odor distracts his senses—offense, that resolve now shall be required for the mere act of consciousness—and of a sudden he cannot be content. 'tis an unsettling addition to a life's recipe.

He backs away into the sun, to end the moment.

"I understand now why you are without sleep."

Orson laughs. "And I well understand why you are not." Silence again intervenes for a time, until Orson again breaks it. "Friend, here is what we shall accomplish this day. Take my bicycle and find Jonathan while I catch my morning's rest. Tomorrow I shall accept my share of the labor. Agreed?"

"Agreed," Skeeter says, having been certain of the outcome of the exchange from the moment he arrived. He finds the bicycle propped against the house and mounts it, unwieldy. He looks back at the window, but Orson has vanished already.

Without artificial transport for years, Skeeter's coordination with the pedals takes time to regain. By and by he makes good speed, the clicking and whirring of last eve's disturbance now a continuous accompaniment to his travels. The contraption sails smoothly enough, through quiet avenues and neighborhoods, where women hang laundry and trade gossip across fences. Moving air kisses the sweat of his face to pleasant coolness; trees and sky remain surreal. Thus is momentary being again complete.

There passes Jonathan's house, always vacant by day. The Turners—Jonathan and his three brothers—are an industrious clan, and the more prosperous for it. All the brothers work for Jonathan, the eldest—he will turn twenty-five at his next birthday—despite the fact that they are still of school age. Truants and dropouts they become under his sway, kings of affluent ignorance, drawn to the salaries and entitlements of villainy.

Skeeter reaches the bridge across the Red River, which bisects the township like a snake embalmed mid-slither. The blue-green flow plods purposeful and massive 'neath the old stone span, primeval as nature herself.

25

Just this side of the bridge stands a tavern he has visited rarely, and always at Orson's insistence. The Turners drink there some evenings, along with others of dubious spirit. This, and the fact that liquor holds no appeal for him, keeps him mostly an exile from the tavern, an outcast from the group of his peers.

As for the other side of the bridge, he does not travel that way often, does not know the people of the east end by name. Little is familiar and safe. He feels something like fear bidding him return home.

But new experience calls from across the river, voice louder today than usual. It dares him to cross.

Last eve's elemental departure is a seed now set to burst.

He presses forth therefore, over the bridge, Orson's bicycle sounds encouraging him with their hypnotic cadence.

The One Who Shrugs

A pure farming community is Moorhead, grown up among the most fertile soils of North America. Yet a great business of farming has none to do with farmers or fields—the refineries, the transporters, flocks of accountants and lawyers, like Father—such that her downtown is labyrinthine as any of the great Eastern cities. 'tis overpowering with vital presence, sum of sight and sound thwarting the clearest mind. Vendors brag wares at every corner. Street performers take the mid-blocks, vying for attention and donation. Smells of diverse breads and meats hang rich in the air...pastry and sausage, fresh beef and bison roasted at the spit.

Skeeter's stomach growls a bit with each shop he passes—he is an admirer of all foods. Therefore, even shrinking under the energy of the place, and having breakfasted recently, he pulls to the side and rummages through his pockets. Yes, over a dollar there, the last of his University stipend.

By and by he is settled at a sidewalk café with sweet gravy dumplings, tea, and a few hours to dispose until noon. The waiter is boisterous friendly, curled moustache revealing proud German heritage. Of greater value, the busy man is absent more than present—Skeeter finds turns of blessed solitude, anonymous among all the diligent people passing by like little tornadoes, each short of time to notice him. 'tis a world of worlds within worlds, joined but deliberately aloof.

A performer makes a place on the street nearby and begins to chant a familiar song, popular among farmers in the taverns…

O yonder township, in thee dwell
Ye sallow dregs of grain
Who grow up bounties, thresh and sell
Of Providence, soil and rain
O man and woman, seed and field
Most precious crop revealed
Hold daughters safe and bounties close
That none your crop may steal…

The lyric brings amusement—for who, Skeeter wonders, shall be inclined to rob a farmer of his crops, a father of his daughters?

Then the new vocation rises to mind and his mood sinks. Though not loath to add thievery to Jonathan's long list of transgressions, Young L'adorsity thus far has been reticent of thought on the matter. He understands a sick sadness that has lurked all morning, the prelude to a fear. Who, tasked with minding hogs, can hope to remain free of filth for long? Only one who ignores the filth comes to benefit of it.

Perhaps mothers of prostitutes weep for their daughters' willfulness; perhaps fathers mourn in stubborn silence.

Perhaps these details fall outside Young L'adorsity's circle of concern. And so he chooses, for a time, to ignore it.

A pack of Sioux businessmen comes and goes, deliberating some pressing matter between them. A well-dressed loner follows close, perhaps a thief looking to snake hand in pocket unnoticed. In another direction walks a pair of Chinese farmers, uncomfortable in formal clothes—they have left their fields for a day of buying and selling.

And here approaches an elderly couple, husband and wife. By their manner and distant-heard accents they are British, dressed as tourists moreover—'tis mysterious as to why any such as these should come to America but for business. Still, here they are, alas; and they intend to take a table at the cafe.

The boisterous waiter, all friendliness removed, approaches with haste and shrill voice. "No, no, no!" His message is clear: service is refused. The husband tries to reason, but another waiter joins with the first. Discouraged, the British leave, smoothing hair and clothes as though the altercation had been at all physical. Perhaps dignity lost leaves one feeling disheveled.

Mouth full of dumplings, Skeeter watches dourly, wondering how people retain the strength to hate the British after so many years. For all the diplomatic intrigues of that shadowy government, what quarrel shall require restaurateurs taking up the fight? It seems more an excuse to vomit hatred with pride, the unsightly contents of a souls' indigestion—thinking them the most beautiful of fruits.

The waiters are stern a moment longer; then they commence camaraderie and celebration. Skeeter ignores them, enjoying for a time the flutist who has replaced the singer at some point in the commotion. Lilting notes slide evenly into the collage of sounds, fine organic offset to the artificiality all around.

By and by the dumplings are consumed, tea sipped cool, and the surroundings—even expertly experienced—sink to tedium. The sun is higher, but not nearly high, as young L'adorsity nods adieu to the waiters. He drops his last remaining coin in the flutist's basket, takes the bicycle from its resting spot at the rail, and pushes it away down a sidewalk too crowded to ride full speed.

One additional event of note occurs on the way to the park. Some distance along, Skeeter encounters a tailor shop, an alchemist shop, and then a little church, tenants as one in adjoining pedantic store fronts. He finds this amusing—help with fashion, help with body and help with spirit, all in the same block.

A man stands in the waning shadow of the building, smoking a pipe and watching Skeeter's halting progress with amusement. He is settled in look, of perhaps fifty years. A well-groomed beard leaves the greater part of his face unobscured. Green eyes, neither sharp nor commanding, are in some way potent beneath a plain fabric hat. And when the man speaks, his voice is hushed, that one must work to hear him in the din.

"You are not of the downtown," the man says, when Skeeter has approached. "Your face is new…"

"Surely you cannot know all of the faces passing. There are so many."

"I aim to know as many as I can. 'tis my calling, in any case."

"You are the alchemist then? Or the preacher?"

"A bit of both, but I claim neither title nor risk of either."

"Oh?" Skeeter comprehends not, but such is the joy of conversation. The answer will come.

"This little chapel is my workplace. And these fair people

of Moorhead are my business."

"Oh."

"Elder Krauss," the man announces, extending a hand. "Elder being my given name, as well as my vocation."

"My given name is Peter L'adorsity. But from ageless youth, Skeeter is my nickname, a shadow that obscures me. I am that infernal bug, scourge of the flatlands."

"Oh, and do the mosquitoes defer from attacking one of their brethren?"

"They do, as a fact." This is a joke, of course; but of a coincidence, his skin is ever free of welts.

"'tis a good thing for you, Skeeter," says the other, and they shake hands. Krauss holds the grip an extra moment before releasing. "Yes, now I understand. You are a curiosity already."

"Why?"

"I sense your life by touch, all blessings and ailments revealed. Many combinations exist, no two alike. But yours..."

"You are outdoors today," Skeeter interrupts. "Is there no business within your church to which you would attend?"

"They do not go in, so I come out."

"None go in?"

"Sadly, no. Times are good, young Skeeter; and when Providence is faithful, men, by nature, feel no inclination to return the favor. The churches, they wither of late. Once, great steeples rose above every township. And now..." He motions at the storefront. "Here is where greatness waits, until needed again."

"Hardly a sensible arrangement. Hope you for bad times then, that the institution may at last prosper?"

"You scoff, but I sense cruelty is not of you. Are you yourself, or has somebody attacked you?" The man leans close. "Tell me verily, what troubles you this day?"

Silence ensues, and there are no birds. Motors, horse

31

hooves and street music meld one perfect and ugly sound. Still, it is not unpleasant. By and by, Skeeter grins and says simply: "Whatever my troubles, most times they feel far."

"An honest answer; I believe this. You are a mystery then, for no man is happy…and you are happy. I fear for you."

"Fear? Why?"

"Because with men, all things pass."

"These are your predictions then? Men's prosperity must pass; even my peace shall depart, that your vocation may blossom anew for our troubles?" Skeeter sighs with the anticlimax, for the conversation had seemed initially promising…

"Take my hand again," Krauss says, "that you understand my motive."

Puzzled, Skeeter complies. The man's grasp is firm with resolve, and something more. Deep, deep, he senses a presence, weakly human, pained, yet grand, tranquil as all healing. He releases and backs away a step. "I understand," he hears himself say.

"What do you understand?"

"That you are pure. Your motives…"

"And how do you know this?"

"I know not how or why. 'tis a natural thing to know, I suppose."

"No. You have a gift, young soul, that rarest of senses beyond the corporal. To possess it is blessed…but it brings a risk, where some knowledge is too much to bear. Tell me again, verily. What troubles you this day?"

Skeeter has found himself entranced these past moments, but now he notices the building's shadow is nearly vanished. High noon comes quickly.

"Thank you for your time, Sir," he says, to dismiss the man. "Now I have business. I am late, I fear, and today is my first day at a new vocation…"

"Oh? What sort of work is it, Peter?"

"I am a messenger."

"Before my...retirement, I was a messenger...a postal agent. Today I remain a messenger of a different sort, for those open to hearing." Then strangely, Krauss' eyes open wide and his face creases with laughter. "The sort of messages you will be delivering, I do not care to know. But I feel something, a new prediction. Today you shall deliver a gift to a person who wants not any gift—a message well beyond the scope of your employ! Ha! I should like to know how things progress..."

Skeeter is puzzled by the last, but this man is long of wind; to explore his thoughts will take time. Another day, perhaps...

The other continues: "You will see me again."

Young L'adorsity nods politely, leaps upon the bicycle and starts, reckless, against the flow of bodies. Progress is slow, but Elder Krauss' knowing laugh melts soon enough into the consommé of city sounds.

Merely a trickster the man must be, out to attract curious patrons to his one-man show—with probing questions and broadly phrased fortune-telling. But a memory of perceived purity is there as well. Perhaps this trickster is virtuous at heart, as one genuinely deluded...

Never having been late to any meeting, Skeeter makes with all resolve for the park where the evil one waits. Traffic thins, by and by. The buildings here are merely functional, their architecture uninspired. Vendors are unseen in any byway. Instead, dogs roam, small packs of them, tails wagging on the hunt for no more sport than garbage.

East Moorhead—the bad side—and ahead lies an anachronism of faded green: the park. To one end a play area for children, swings and sandboxes, deserted with schools in

33

session. To the other, an outbuilding, a grove of young trees useless for shade—and men lurk, surly presences suggesting no good intention.

The men, four of them, are dressed one and the same in black, as though mourning long-departed innocence. They stare at the bicycle with dull eyes, feigning disinterest.

One of them Skeeter recognizes as Jonathan's younger brother, Matthew, his fiery red hair a family paradox, walnut-brown being the sibling norm. The father travels oft' on business; perhaps this is a good explanation, if never mentioned in polite company.

Jonathan himself is nowhere to be seen.

Matthew's lip curls with distaste at Skeeter's arrival. "L'adorsity," he says, coldly.

"Indeed, Matthew. And your brother Jonathan?"

"Why do you ask?"

"We are to meet at this very place," Skeeter tells him. "I am in his employ."

"I know nothing of any meeting, and nothing of this employment of which you speak. I am in Jonathan's employ—I, these men, and certainly not you."

Another man, unfamiliar, comes near. He is large, stocky, perhaps thirty-five years old, an air of apathetic kindness hiding an indiscernible center. "Ignore this one," he says easily, shrugging toward Matthew. "Jonathan told us of your coming. You are Orson?"

Skeeter extends a hand and they shake. "I am Skeeter. Orson and I are…interchangeable."

The man shrugs and turns away without introducing himself. "You are early. Listen, Jonathan comes."

A horse indeed approaches, but soon it is clear that Jonathan is not the rider. Instead a farmer, from his style of dress, approaches from the northern lands beyond the township.

He brings the animal near, to call to the men. "Hello. May we do business?"

"If business be what you seek," answers the one who shrugs.

"You deal in the finer pleasures, so I have heard."

"This is possible. Which is your pleasure, light or dark?"

"Light, dark, blond, redhead: I am not a fastidious taker at first inquiry."

"A fortunate circumstance for all. Where is your farm, sir?"

"The North Road, second farmstead past the brook."

"Very well. Expect a visitor soon, and may she be a pleasant surprise."

"And the price?"

"As you are acquainted with these finer pleasures, you shall also be acquainted with their price."

Satisfied, the farmer gallops off to prepare the arrival of a prostitute at his home, however one accomplishes such a thing. Hide the family pictures, perhaps, away on holiday as they are. Poor husband, remaining a few days more to look after the milking, surely deserves a finer pleasure now and again.

Matthew fetches his bicycle from the grass, ready to deliver the message. But the one who shrugs conceives a new notion. He points at Skeeter. "You, as you claim, are in Jonathan's employ. Ready to begin, are you?"

"Let us begin," Skeeter answers, a sudden hint of angst tingling his stomach.

"Very well. Remember you what the farmer said?"

Skeeter recites the farmer's location.

The other scribbles a house number on a scrap of paper, hands it to Skeeter. "Here is the girl. Her name is Lauren. Find Lauren and send her to the farmer."

Skeeter looks at the paper. "She is here? Is this her

35

home? Or a business?"

"Simply find the girl, and send her to the farmer."
Brusqueness shows in the man's voice. "Go now, lest I send
Matthew in your stead."

Skeeter nods, the other shrugs, Matthew sulks, and young
L'adorsity is off, racing in search of a street he knows not where
to find. Once out of sight of the others, he stops to pray help
from a passerby. After a time he is facing the right direction,
making all speed for the girl's location.

He finds the house, finds the girl and, suddenly and
completely, loses consciousness.

Luz

Fright, Dear Reader! Never shall a man's first choice be to lie helpless on a strange floor, lacking barest control of mind and body. Thank what blessings exist that Skeeter suffers not embarrassment of lost bowels as well at that moment, for such is the magnitude of shock that fells him.

Let us return to moments prior, that all may comprehend what has transpired. Young L'adorsity locates the place straight away, a rural neighborhood much like his own, but on the far side of town. The house is typical as well, a faded two-story of the sort often carved into small apartments by greedy landlords. He coasts onto the dirt yard. Two women lounge on a wide porch, but when he asks after a girl named Lauren, he is directed around the house, to the back.

Impassive horses occupy stables at the rear of the property, saddles thrown over timber fences. There is a small guest cottage nearby where, 'neath the shade of a tattered awning, a bare door hangs ajar.

He knocks, and a woman's voice bids him enter. Some small trepidation overtakes him— not for fear, but for the possibility of a rude mistake on his part, this being a woman's private place. Watchful, he steps through the entry. Away from noon's bright, features of a small drawing room swim in his eyes. The decorating is elaborate, charming, if a bit jumbled, as though someone began it with earnest only to lose heart at a point. The smells are charming as well: the musty decay that lingers after a rainy season; and over that the distinctive aura of woman, her powders, her soaps and colognes.

Skeeter has never stood within an unmarried woman's home; the sensation of trespass is briefly exciting.

Noises come from another room; he turns to the sound. The lady looks 'round the corner at him, hair of lightest auburn or zinfandel—falling perfect straight as a living unity, every move of it seamless and right. He is dizzy…

A little girl plays in a sandbox, painted wooden doll in hand, singing. Five years old, hair perfect straight, eyes powder blue—and she is full of the moment.

Her child voice sings, and a young boy listens nearby, sharing in its perfection. Life becomes grand in this wildish yard, of grasses and rocks beneath a great sticky tree.

Savage! A big boy like a shadow appears and snatches the doll, holding it high, laughing, taunting. No singing now, only the sad sound of her wailing. The boy listening rises gracefully. Life becomes rage in this wildish yard.

A stone arcs with uncanny aim. It strikes the big boy at the temple. He howls and runs, and the doll bounces to the ground. The girl-child has her doll again, but there is no more singing.

All is as it was, but nevermore as it was.

"Are you dead sir? Shall I summon an undertaker?" A voice of lovely mist, speaking nonsense. "Awake, sir!"

Skeeter wakes, finds a face before him. That face, so much older. Thin lips, narrow nose and chin, powder blue eyes, her hair ever the same.

"I know you," he says. When he sees that he is supine, he rises quickly, the drawing room whirling around him still.

"Why are you here?" she asks. "And why did you faint?"

"I fell…not normal for me."

"I should hope not. Perhaps some water…"

"Water, yes. Thank you."

She moves to fetch the water, no urgency in her step. Her manner is oddly detached.

Briefly alone, he takes a place on the worn sofa, trying to dispose himself—for the deepest sadness now weighs upon his body. Tears well up and he gasps to subdue them. O torture, the pain consumes every inch of him!

The woman brings a tall glass, overflowing, small fingers wet from it. She stands passively, watching him take it in gulps.

"Perhaps the heat was my undoing," he says, after a time—trying to hide all emotion, but with voice still breaking. Then stronger: "I rode here with some haste."

"Who are you?"

He looks up to meet her eyes. "You are Luz."

She makes a sudden motion, as though an invisible fist has struck her hard at the forehead. Color spills from her face and she stares long at him, eyes wide.

Then, as one shrugging off an offense, she recovers. "I am Lauren."

"Jonathan," Skeeter breathes. "'twas Jonathan that took your doll. Two years older, and bigger than you and I both…"

She ignores the comment. "You are a messenger; may I guess?"

He grasps her wrist, that she heed him. "And I who threw the stone…"

But with touch comes knowing; he suffers the emptiness of her, as in her very bones. Her body and soul, so young, shrink away, tender humors choked in bitterness.

Their eyes are met, and not a glint of understanding crosses between them. Silence, a savage contest, a tense vacuum of a moment. She wins. She throws his hand from her wrist. Like a sorceress, she summons indignant tone, voice without tremor. "Cross you my threshold, faint at my feet—and now comes this nonsense? My name is Lauren, not Luz, and I have never met you. Explain your business here, or leave."

"I am Skeeter." He brightens, spontaneous laugh at his lips. "The years…ever so many you are lost to me. And now…"

Weakly resolute, she stands silent, face revealing none but fatigue. She points him to the door.

What more to say, he knows not. She does not hear…

To the door then, face grim, still holding the glass. At the last he sighs, turns, and tells her: "The North Road, second farmstead past the brook…a farmer waits." He hates his mouth for speaking, his legs for carrying him here."

"Oh," she answers, emotionless.

"I am the messenger."

"So you are. Was a price named?"

He shakes his head. "A new client, it appears. Perhaps discretion limited discussion."

She reaches to take the glass. "And now I have a message for you, Peter. Hear me; you are not to come this way again. Tell them to send that dolt Matthew."

Dismissed, he is out. The door slams. For a moment he stands lifeless, as a package of discarded refuse. Emotions clash until his head rings with the conflict—so much import to each side of a feeling, such that it all sums to a great nothing of nausea.

The bicycle glints in the sun, beckoning dignity. He finds the handlebars and glides away through surreal day, the mighty sun a dark tingling shadow.

Sadness lingers ever severe, the ache after the sting. What to do?

'tis best to seek numbness in such times, he decides, and so he shoves these new troubles into a dark place he has created of late. "Silly girl," he states out loud. He tries to laugh carefree. He listens to the sounds, wonders at the odd people zooming past in the street. He vows to lie in the grass for a time when he reaches the park. A calm exhale and all will be well again. But the pedals of Orson's machine are leaden beneath his feet. He is not confident.

The wooden doll lies forgotten on the grass. The young boy remembers the sandbox. He looks, and the girl child is not there.

He senses her. High, high up in the sticky tree...she perches like a bird on a branch, knees drawn to her chin, calmly observing the back yard's activities. He moves to climb the tree, but finds legions of crawling things, marching vertical toward the sweet fruit.

"Ants! Yew!"

She sees him and and climbs still higher. Therefore he braves the ants, and skitters determinedly up the sticky trunk, grabbing hand-holds, heaving and leaping. He comes just beneath where she sits. She has the good thick branch; he takes a lighter one nearby. It sags beneath his weight.

"Bad boy..."

She has spoken, at last. He follows her gaze, to the far

41

side of the yard, where boys and girls are playing loudly. The boy with a bruise at his temple now dominates the group, calling out commands in a shrill voice.

"Bad boy," young Peter agrees.

There is a crack, and the branch gives way. He is falling, arms flailing. He catches a branch, nearly saves himself, but loses grip, spinning to the ground in a cloud of torn leaves.

The hard blow has taken his breath. He gasps, after a time finding stubborn air—he is distracted by a new sound. The little girl is laughing, voice of music, nearly perfect as her singing. It goes on and on. Once he is able, he laughs too, and all is complete. Lying on his back he can see her through gaps in the branches, joyful lips, hair perfect straight.

Men stand in the park as before. But now another rider has come; a man clothed in heavy blue fabric—inappropriate for the heat—speaks at length to the men from atop his horse. Skeeter supposes it is Jonathan, but at the last moment finds that it is not. The one who shrugs catches glimpse of Skeeter approaching and shrugs violently, motioning without arms. Come no closer, is the message. So Skeeter curves aside, nonchalant, to avoid meeting them. Chancing a look back, he sees that the visitor is a constable, come to harass the wrongdoers.

He stops at a distance to wait, wondering if perhaps he ought simply to give up and go home. But no, resolve survives even in this strange day. By and by one of the men leaves; 'tis Matthew, riding angry on his bicycle, red hair gaudy in the sun. To University where he belongs, obviously. The constable concludes his discourse and departs as well, so Skeeter returns to work. The one who shrugs nods a casual greeting.

"Trouble with the law?" Skeeter asks, dropping cross-legged to the grass to rest.

"Irritation, merely. Jonathan's method infuriates them."

"His method?"

"We who wait, the clients who know us, the girls we know…the messengers who change faces ever so frequent—and you believed you were hired for your talents, ha! A constable should need track these chameleons each to his destination to learn of all the girls' diverse locations."

"The constables must know what you do, else why pester you?"

"They know. Too lazy and hindered by formalities they are, ever to land a single charge."

"Surely not all are lazy…"

The other shrugs. "The industrious ones, Jonathan pays a share, and all continues as it will. Jonathan is a brilliant man, you shall learn. Audacious, and with a kinder spirit than most."

Both turn at the sound of another customer approaching.

The day's labor, it appears, must continue.

Children march in an uneven queue along the gravel road. Ahead towers their headmaster, busily leading the way; and beyond him towers a monstrous structure, slate gray in the distant haze. The grain refinery—every township has one—is the destination of this class trip. As it dominates the skyline, so its presence looms even in the lives of these students, most headed for the farming life.

Six-year-old Peter, trudging mid-line, is distracted by a feminine energy behind him. Remembering the girl, he slows his pace, letting others pass, until she is at his side—for she has been lingering at the rear of the group. She walks silent for a time, seemingly oblivious to him—then she reaches for his hand, delicate fingers closing tight around his. He is electrified at the touch. The world disappears, all awareness of anything but her soft skin.

"Silly," she says, impassive, but he can feel her smile. In that moment he learns, for all time, the meaning of perfection.

Beast

What ill-conceived choice it was, envelops young L'adorsity within this circumstance, relentlessly as innocent misstep leads to fall. Gravity, impartial universal, it craves our flesh, draws men ever down. And oh, what tumble the wise child has embarked upon, he knows little.

For with men, all things pass—even, we shall see, the delicate safeties of sanity and future.

This day should have been free of consequence—such was the plan—but for the new awareness he has acquired upon recognizing Luz. Aiming at perhaps small enticement, he has struck confusion instead—made ever so urgent by connection to those powerful memories. To see every soul as child most innocent—inevitably to mourn what has come—is to lose heart in the deception that brought him here. His circle of concern is widened. He cannot ignore the filth upon him.

Various strangers comprise the remainder of the day's visits, half-dozen prostitutes scattered about the township. Each woman he meets feels more haunted than the last. Lisa, the blonde; Ellen the Negro; Ann the Sioux; Sandra, a second blonde; Mary, brunette; and Tsi, a stunning princess, enigmatic in race. To each he delivers similar intelligence, fresh direction to some sublimely bad place, as though none could find the well-trod path of ruin unaided.

Ruin of a particular sort it must be; for how else is Jonathan to profit?

The man himself at last pays a visit to the park nearly at dusk, having promised noon. He comes not atop trusty steed, but riding something none expected, even those most acquainted with him.

A honk echoes up and down the avenue. All present in the park turn and, behold! A monstrous vehicle approaches with Jonathan smiling proudly at the wheel. The automobile gleams as gold in the yellow streetlamps, its skin mysteriously translucent. It produces less of a racket than most cars, a lighter odor as well; perhaps it is a more advanced type.

Having no friends who can afford such contraptions, Skeeter knows little of them.

The normally subdued criminals whoop as their leader brings the beast to rest among them, mighty wheels carving ruts in the grass. Jonathan hops out directly, for the top of the vehicle is open, canvas cover folded at the rear.

"She is a 2001 model Stallion Renegade," he announces. "And she will outpace the fastest horse any day you try." Cries of "How much?" ensue, to which he replies, "Under two thousand, a bargain, from Reinhold's shop by the Red River."

He crosses to the front and raises the bonnet, revealing what appears a slab of solid refined metal, a maze of cables and

46

odd-shaped boxes. All are impressed with the workmanship, allowing that not a one has the least comprehension of its functioning.

Skeeter recalls his physics from University, yet cannot muster an interest in the mechanics of the thing. He waits, back of the group, wanting only to be paid and relieved.

Business, brisk by day, seems to dwindle with dusk—owing perhaps to early-rising farmers being the primary clientele—and so the workday appears finished. Eventually the spell of the new toy subsides and Jonathan remembers to complete the business for which he came. He consults a large pocket watch, then begins paying each of the men from a roll in his pocket, taking great ceremony in the pulling, straightening and counting of each note.

At last he looks to Skeeter, noticing him for the first time. "L'adorsity, old friend, 'tis good that you have come," he says with exaggerated geniality. "As you see, this business is simple to learn, lucrative for any who are devoted to its smooth operation—you arrived at noon, did you?"

Skeeter nods. The one who shrugs, listening nearby, confirms. Jonathan peels seven green-brown bills and hands them over, the money slimy with the sweat of his trouser pocket.

"Drinks?" Jonathan motions inclusively. "Good men prowl the taverns when labors are done."

"Home for me, a waiting supper, quiet eve…"

"Yes, of course. Grandmother has much to tell of her day, no doubt."

Shrugger raises an eyebrow, not having absorbed until now that the two are of long history. Jonathan turns away, obligatory motions complete—snickers to be withheld until the odd one departs. With not another word Skeeter leaps on the bicycle, sole ally of the day.

DS Swanson

The ride home is easy as a downhill feeling, speed's breeze upon his face. Sunset is climaxed to burnt reds and ambers. The dim lit windows of home smile friendly when at last he turns the final corner.

At dinner, he proudly presents Father with four of the dollars, keeping the other three for spending. The old man, reviewing case work at the table, grunts appreciation, nearly meeting his son's eyes for an instant. 'tis a brief good moment, with Mother looking blankly on, and Grandmother looking simply blank.

After dishes are cleaned and stowed, Skeeter travels on foot to Orson's. The shades of the oversized window are open. An electric light arcs intense against the impending gloom, so that the bedroom stands like a display case for the neighborhood's inspection. A small party is in progress, this eve as nearly every. Though not many can fit in an average bedroom, half-dozen young men and women are leaned against walls or lounged on the bed, gripping glasses of yellow-brown liquid. Vigorously they ignore the fussing moths and beetles attracted by the light; instead they discuss various matters which they seem to find urgently amusing.

Orson sits at the bureau, sipping a tumbler of lager. "The bicycle survives?" he asks, first thing when Skeeter steps through the window. The others ignore him.

"Yes, a trusty machine, much appreciated."

"Where is it?"

"I should like to keep it a bit longer."

"Pray tell, why?" Orson offers Skeeter a glass of the ale, as he does nearly every evening. The other stuns him by accepting it, his first in over a year.

Skeeter sniffs the drink, sips. "Let us amble about for a time out of doors."

And so they go together out the window, across the yard

48

and along the street. Night gathers full, cricket sounds rising, and Skeeter realizes the day's tension by its leaving. Only that desperate sadness remains in him.

"Life would come easy, were all empathy removed," he says. Hearing this aloud from his own lips, he realizes its truth.

"Empathy?" Orson gently scoffs. "Friend, you have made a good start this eve; do not ruin it with your musing. Drink your beer and all will be well. But do tell why you need the bicycle..."

"I believe you ought not work for Jonathan," Skeeter says. "I will work for a time, I myself. Might you agree?"

Orson groans, feigning agony over the matter, then: "Very well. I've another offer, even so, from the grain refinery. 'tis rebuilt since the last disaster, with new safety in mind."

"Please be careful..."

"'tis near enough that I am willing to walk there; you may use the bicycle indefinitely. But, regarding Jonathan's enterprises, I am curious. Is it for love of the work or hate of it that you ask me to shun his employ?"

Skeeter laughs suddenly to ward off the question. "How many times, suppose you, have Jonathan and I fought?"

Orson whistles. "A lifetime of it, at the least. It would have continued daily had you not lost more often than winning. I myself gave it up after he beat me severely—I have long forgiven him for that." He eyes Skeeter sidelong in the gloom. "Is that it, then? You see fit to forge a friendship with the man? 'tis excellent, and long in coming. I am pleased that my efforts have succeeded to the benefit of all..."

"Might you recall the time, ever so long ago, I struck out with a flung stone, bruising his head?"

A moment of dreamy pondering, and Orson replies: "I believe I witnessed the aftermath of that. Were we four years of age, you and I; five perhaps? You, outdoors in the back yard; I,

49

in the house to steal an early snack—that girl's mother cooked lovely raisin spice cookies, best in the neighborhood. Do you remember them?"

"Persimmon as well, fresh of the tree," Skeeter adds. "She gathered us to her one and all, ever adoring of children."

"Fine woman, yes. And our own mothers…glad to be rid of us for the day."

"My point being, that I cast the stone at Jonathan because he was hurting the young girl. I saved her."

"Yes, Jonathan was a brute. The size of him…goodness."

"Do you recall the girl's name?"

"Yes, of course. An odd name…Luz. What full-blooded German is given a Latin name? But it comes to me easily, for a fond memory I hold. She once showed us her private parts…"

"What!"

"You saw none of that? Perhaps your mother held you home a day. It happened in the barren lot nearby… 'twas the first time I'd set eyes upon the likes of that, and thankfully not the last."

Skeeter sighs, gags another sip of the ale from the glass he still carries. "Are you aware of what has become of her?"

"The family moved, early, I know not where. Boston, France, another neighborhood here in Moorhead—what difference to children of that age?" Orson stops walking, curiosity overtaking him. "Why are you focused upon this? Has something stirred your memory?"

Skeeter briefly hears the crickets and the trees and all of the night screaming: "DO NOT TELL HIM!" But the voices of reason are meager amid the new din of his mind.

"Have you seen her?" Orson's numb intellect is assembling the clues. "You have…"

"I saw a girl resembling the one we knew. But she denied knowing me. Why?" Recalling the moment, Skeeter is awash again in the same feelings. He shakes his head and squints, of puzzlement and frustration. "I am sure she lied—I called myself Skeeter, and later she called me Peter, as if we were children still. She knows only my given name…"

Orson grows steadily more astonished and ecstatic all the while Skeeter is speaking. Suddenly he laughs loudly, slapping knees and spinning about. "Oh, this is priceless! Our little friend is here in Moorhead and she is a…" He lowers his voice. "She is a prostitute?"

Skeeter is appalled at the other's reaction. But Orson carries on, long and loud, until young L'adorsity is compelled to walk a line away from him.

After a time, Orson follows. "Look here, you. What is the matter?"

Skeeter turns and stares hard, but cannot muster as much passion outside as in. He mutters simply: "It is not funny."

"Of course it is funny," Orson declares blithely.

A sudden desire by one best friend to strike the other comes and passes. When Skeeter speaks again, each word emerges slowly and with great weight: "You marvel as a rare jewel at this first-rate bit of scandal. But what joy be in it, save the sadistic sort which dishonors he who finds it? You are seduced by…the perfume of a poor girl's life blood rushing out. She is grown, and with the air of a lovely corpse. For all your concern, you are even as much killing her yourself."

Orson is silenced, utterly, for once. He stands a moment, trying to comprehend the other's rare outburst.

Then he takes the remainder of his glass with one gulp. "Hear, hear."

Skeeter, after a spell, lightens. "Hear, hear," he repeats, and downs his drink as well, swallowing hard to quash a belch.

"A toast for the lady," Orson says, with an over-furtive glance. "Or perhaps a moment of silence…"

51

"Anything will do."

Orson points at a nearby house. "I believe this is the place, is it not? She lived here. Look, the sandbox in the back."

"You've lost your bearings again. The house stands the next street over."

"You are mistaken. There is the persimmon tree."

"That is an oak."

A benign argument begins, distracting friends from their true angers. By and by words run thin. Orson takes Skeeter's empty glass. "Let us rejoin the party. Perhaps another drink be adequate to soothe your damaged spirit."

The two walk back to Orson's house, where little has changed. Skeeter refuses another drink.

Undiscouraged, Orson leans near. "I believe I spied lust in these ladies' eyes when you arrived tonight." He indicates the female revelers, none of whom show slightest interest. "Try your luck…"

"My thoughts are intent on varied matters this eve. I shall leave you to your celebration, old friend, whatever purpose it may serve you."

"Perhaps that is for the best…"

They bid one another good eve, Orson wearing an unreadable expression. He glances back frequently as young L'adorsity leaves.

Walking home, Skeeter detours to look for the girl's old house, finds it with little trouble. Lights are on: a new family resides here, new children to climb the sticky persimmon tree— hopefully not to fall. Not wishing to disturb, he stretches to view the back yard from the street, but the dim is impenetrable.

He abandons the place and returns home. The rest of his family has retired for the evening.

For the first time in memory, bedtime is torture, sleep a

far-flung destination.

He tries to enjoy the dark, but thinks only of Luz. He cannot imagine her face as it is, for he only saw her briefly; the child persists in memory. So he grapples with merely the idea of her, as though essence can create a visage of its own being.

She is a ghost babbling at his ear unceasing. In time he is defeated, sanity overwhelmed.

He becomes a want without a mind.

His first intention of the night is to go and find her.

Gelding

For once, Orson's bicycle lends no aid. The clicking sound has been a misadjusted gear all along; Skeeter learns of this when, barely a block into the journey, the chain breaks and trails on the ground behind him. He stops, observes the situation with stoic acceptance, then pushes the crippled thing home, to stow it in the back yard.

On foot it shall be then. He makes the trudge across the span of the township, hugging tranquility tight, against a choir chanting stanzas of impulse and bafflement. The river, the downtown, the park; they march ever so slowly now. By the time he arrives at her neighborhood, his thoughts alone have made him weary. He knows not what he will accomplish with this visit. At the least, he will expose her lie; learn why she acknowledged him not. And even in advance of these, the practical matters worry him more. Will she be home? Will she speak? Will she be alone?

The last is the worst, for a most unwieldy scene it will present, and frustration to have traveled far only to earn embarrassment.

And so, praying to Providence that the woman is unaccompanied, he stands at last under the awning, shadow of which now forms utter dark within night. The door is closed, but a candle burns within, its flicker passing through a shaded window. He knocks lightly, waits; knocks a second time. Nearby, horses are restless for his unsanctioned presence in the yard.

Door open, she is before him, ever so brief. A look, a groan, and she disappears again, leaving the door ajar.

Unsure, he calls softly, "Pray that I may enter?"

Her voice emanates from within, speaker now unseen. "Scarce can I stop you. Enter in; attend to what business you must."

He complies, and sees the parlor as before, but by candlelight. The charming smells are now laced with the medicine tang of alcohol. Bottles litter the foot table, one empty, one half-full with amber whiskey, and one of merlot. She is undecided as to poisons this eve. The lady herself is crumpled upon the small couch, wearing bedclothes and a robe. Whether she has been sleeping, or waiting to sleep, is unclear. Her hair, straight as always, splays across ruddy freckles, over eyes deliberately closed—a final stubborn denial of him.

"Luz," he says… "Luz". He takes a seat at the end of the couch, lifting her feet to make room. After a time, he speaks again. "Dear, I am ever so glad to see you."

Finally, she speaks, eyes edging half open. "Why?" And he is not certain of the answer to that. She moves, reaches at the bottle to take whiskey directly from its cheerless round mouth. Then she glares at him, and slurs: "Have you come to see my private parts again, old friend?"

His jaw drops, but he answers quickly. "I have never seen you...this I swear. I was not present for those events."

"Always a first time," she moans, failing seductiveness in her intoxication.

"You believe this is what I seek?"

A tired sigh, then she catches him in a crooked gaze. "'tis what all men seek. Somewhere amid all your concern, all the loving speech that I can sense welling within you, this motive shall also be ready to spring. Therefore let us save time and speech. Make your business that you may be sated...that you leave me to my dark home and solitude."

Her directness stuns him. No response is at his lips, and any forming within mind suddenly rings too flat to consider voicing.

"I have no answer, dear, but that I am troubled," he says, attempting candor. "Something is lost that needs recovery. We need simply to talk, you and I."

"As I said already, let talk be spare, for I am an expert in my craft. You know not what I have seen in my travels, silly boy. Your own body you comprehend not, as I, simply from experience. I know places of you—a lifetime within arm's reach, and you miss them entirely—wonderful sensations, that you be inspired to scream 'My love forever!' All for a breath; then the fated change, goodbye and escape, for your loins are your master. All my loves are star-crossed. Pity, pity, love, how callous you are."

It occurs to him that she is drunk beyond conversing. He sighs, troubling not to speak again.

And then, of all things, the moment feels right, silence being the required ingredient. He is content for the first time in hours.

After a time, her breathing becomes even, as alcohol is a

mighty sedative. He rests a hand on one of her bare feet, enjoying its warmth, and loses himself in the flickering of the candle. The flame dances fitfully, disturbed by runny wax collecting at its feet. Eventually it finds way back to stable form, and the light of the room is even.

A hopeful drama…that life should resolve so evenly.

Later she wakes, looks at him with blank eyes, takes another gulp of the whiskey and passes to sleep within the instant. A lyric enters his consciousness, whose tune he cannot recall. In this moment the words seem fitting…

> *Slender twig, which bends when shaken*
> *Woman spirit, holy matron*
> *At cold winds' strong assail,*
> *Does sway, malleable and frail*
> *'till winter sees the naked tree*
> *Autumn's auburn leaves*
> *Surrendered to the cunning breeze*

He is reluctant to end this good time, but there is duty to see her safely to bed and to make his way home. He delays perhaps another half hour, then sets to making this happen.

"Rise, dear. I must go now." The girl does not rise. Perplexed, he keeps trying to wake her, to no avail.

At last he tries scooping her up to carry her to the bed, but she is heavy in spite of her light build. He sits defeated for a moment.

"I shall need a horse to haul you, love."

At that point a most dangerous course of action is born. It comes, as most bad things do, in the form of an idea, a flash of insightful incitement. For minutes on end he speaks to the idea, entertained more than entranced. It pursues him aggressively, charming and tempting him. Inevitably he is seduced…

57

The horses stand sleepy in the pen outside. He finds the proper saddle, one etched with her alias, Lauren, and checks girths to determine which horse is hers. He finds one of matching size, a tall gelding, and sets about making acquaintance with the animal. An apple would be ideal; but some time spent stroking the mane and meeting the animal's gaze proves sufficient. After saddling the horse, he leads him to a spot adjacent to the door.

The difficult work is next. Aware that a man should be capable of lifting a woman, Skeeter sees the problem as one of determination. Perhaps, he was unsure before, whether to leave her where she lay, and that indecision weakened him. Now he has no doubt. Human will is a mighty force of nature; and so he strains and manages to rise straight with her limp form sprawled across the front of him, like a mother carrying a giant child. He eases backward, blows out the candle and leaves the darkened room, shutting the door behind him with a hook of his leg.

The gelding has no pity for his predicament, standing high and proud. He simply cannot lift this woman over his head. A moment's thought, another moment, and suddenly he heaves one foot into the stirrup, a hand 'round the saddle horn, and his grounded leg jumps with all its might. A yell, a miracle, and up they go as one; he comes to rest in the saddle with the sleeping girl facing backward, her head lolling heavy on his shoulder. She comes briefly alive at the disturbance, berating him with mumbled nothings, then drifts away. Somewhere a dog barks, and then there is silence.

Satisfied as he has ever been, he takes one more look at her now-empty abode. Then he spurs the horse forward for the long and bumpy ride home.

Classes are dismissed for the day, and seven-year-old Peter wanders home. Movements purposeful, graceful,—yet always defying others' understanding—he zigs and zags across the neighborhood, perhaps as the first explorers traveled across this great continent. He is always alone.

This day, a trap is set. A shadow rises up across his path: that big boy, a few years older, and many pounds heavier. The enemy is not alone. A band of accomplices spreads at either side like jaws of a pincer, to surround its prey. The seven-year-old continues toward them, within them, quietly wondering how much pain the next few moments possibly can contain.

Savage blows commence, amazing forces, each disrupting consciousness for a brief second. The ground jumps up to slap him harder, and he tastes dirt, curious flavor to distract from kicks landing at his ribs.

A new pair of footsteps approaches and a sound rises up like an animal, a battle cry. The punishment stops abruptly. Light of day returns, for bodies are flying and falling; grunts and cries all around. The criminals disappear one by one, fleeing for life.

The seven-year-old rolls and gazes up at the lone silhouette standing over him.

"Silly Peter, have you no fear at all?" Batiste, seventeen-year-old brother, pulls the younger to his feet. "You should have run."

"Heroes deserve their rewards," the seven-year-old answers, wiping dirt from swollen lips. "Long has this day waited for me…"

Luz

She wakes a few hours before dawn, on the bed next to him, still clad in night clothes and robe. Perhaps nature calls her awake, for, after the initial shock she displays—might such surprises be common in her vocation?—she is quick to ask after the plumbing. Skeeter shows her along the hall to the water closet, and returns to his room to await her.

He is short on sleep this eve, having made the ride, unloaded his fair prize, and spent the balance of the time watching her sleep—not for obsession or awe, but perhaps a wistful fascination at the divine child spirit lost within her shell, ever linked in kinship with his own being. To recapture that nameless substance in her and in him, to animate it anew, to share it freely…this now seems his greatest wish.

For her face glimmers ever hopeful in slumber, restored

and complete. He wonders and wonders…what shall it take to look upon such peace by day?

She does not return from the water closet, and so he goes looking, finds her outdoors in his front yard. The moon is set, and a fog uncharacteristic of Moorhead is descending chill and profuse. No lights burn in any home nearby, for no good person is awake in this hour. He stands at the open door; watching her shadowed form for a time. Then he comes alongside her, bare feet swishing on the dewed grass. Together they stand gazing at the nothing. In the anonymity of mutual blindness, her face safe from his sight, a means is found toward conversation beyond a lie.

"Our old neighborhood," she intones.

"Indeed. Your childhood home, two corners and south."

"I recall where I left it. Never have I returned; never would I, but for you bringing me here. Were we not acquainted from birth, I should report you as a kidnapper."

"Were kidnapping my sport, I should feel cheated by the ease of it, my drunken prize."

"Easy or not, your labors are wasted; I shall return home at first light. I work for Jonathan. As it seems, you are in his employ as well."

"No more, for Jonathan is a hidden man; greed propels all his works. He misuses you. He corrupts me. We must be away, you and I, as only this will save us."

"Silly. Jonathan saved me."

"Saved you?" Skeeter stares at her outline, her features nightmarish black on black.

"I am long tainted," she says, "while you grow here in your perfect shell. Still un-hatched you are, little chick, while I am…mature in my shame. It suits me, like an ugly dress that wears just right. 'tis my own to be, and to be well, the one epithet that describes me best. Do you know the word? Can you

61

say it aloud?"

"A mere second's dreaming be ample to gather up...so many excellent words to suit you, dear. The word on your tongue is the last word on mine."

"You know me little to deny what I say. In your mind lives a spirit from your youth, one whose coming of age you never saw. You never missed me, never questioned where I went..."

"How could I, a child myself? I know not even the year of your flight. But yesterday I saw you, was struck flat with the memory. How shall you imagine yourself forgotten?"

"'twas curious, your reaction, to faint at the sight of me..."

"Not surprise, but a great pain I felt."

"Pain? For what?"

"I know not, for I do not judge you. But I regret..."

"Ah, regret, the kindest of words," she answers, voice becoming coarse. "Always the ones who cannot discern empathy from judgment. You believe you care for me, but such help has come before, offered freely—its price a deception. I tell you, Jonathan knows me not...yet he accepts what he sees. Let him profit as he wishes; 'tis life's way. In my eyes he saves me... "

He finds her wrist, squeezes it, sensing her sad energy. "I shall save you from him, even as before with a stone to his head. Perhaps this time a blade to the throat be needed to put him down, that he loose you from these bonds."

"Fierce words," she mocks, "from one who injures not even flies. Where hides this blade you will use?"

He considers it. "Indeed, my first proposal, escape, shall be the more realistic."

"Escape? Hear me, Peter; there is no escape."

"Why?"

"You—in my life but a day—claim to divine my deepest

needs? You are deranged, impetuous of youth's folly. What shall it take to send you away?"

"If you send me away, I shall obey," he says, unsure of his verity. "But I pray you, take time, respecting my thoughts I share. If I am impetuous, are you not over-wary for reasons in common? We are the same age."

"Age, in years—Let us see which of us is the simpler." She shifts her tone, to one patently suggestive. "We've a few hours before dawn. Shall we retire to your virgin bed, innocent man? Perhaps you need simply to be corrupted as all others, that you comprehend life's plainest truths."

He sighs. "Your tone is familiar, heard a few hours ago in your drunk. You think to make any man yours with this voice? All to be your geldings, but with essential parts intact?"

"I mean no such thing—but if this is your wish, take me and be finished."

"Even if I believed you want me for pleasure's sake…you snuffed that flame earlier…by certain words you spoke."

"Certain words…I shall never recall. What wisdom did my drunken lips invent?"

"That if I lay with you, I be of a vile species you despise. Never shall I seek to be despised by you."

She sighs. "You are a hopeless cause."

"The neighborhood stands in agreement."

"Let us retire and sleep as babes, therefore, that morning come quickly and liberate me from your nattering."

Skeeter feels amused by the exchange, once it is ended.

She marches to the front door without another word and he follows her to the indoors, where Father's snores come from one room, Grandmother's from another. What place shall this be for entertaining a lady? Ridiculous, her suggestion…insincere as well. He slumps onto his bed; she joins him, back turned.

This time sleep takes him quickly for exhaustion's sake.

63

Dreams come to entertain him—dreams of her, of childhood's simplicity, of momentary joys beyond control or account. People appear and disappear in such swoony world, even as night and day may come and go unnoticed. In the tactile life of pure unexamined experience, flickering love 'tween souls is ever open and constant. Her songs, her hair…they pass at sunset to the other side of the world; yet so long as day exists somewhere, he will love her.

These things carry him well past the dawn—for the night is fully misted, the morning a diffuse gray radiance insufficient to wake either of them.

Many hours later comes Mother's voice. "Peter…oh, there you are."

He looks up, groggy. "I do not often sleep late."

"True."

"Grandmother…"

"Cleaned and breakfasted. The animals as well."

"You are a dear," he says.

Mother is strenuously deliberate in ignoring Luz's presence. An occasion so infrequent that a parent thinks not to voice a rule against it; yet here is this slight, lovely woman in the good son's bed, albeit fully clothed. A good start; a first time for everything; some such thought undoubtedly passes through Mother's mind.

Skeeter sees but a nervous twitching of the old woman's eye, so he brings the matter to light. "I found an old friend, and bid her find rest here."

"Oh?"

"You remember the neighbor girl, Luz?"

"Yes, yes," says Mother, and her face says no, no.

"Might we have toast?"

"Certainly, dear."

Mother leaves to prepare the snack, glad to be done with the moment. Luz, having been feigning sleep, turns over to face him. She rolls her eyes. "Your mother. All the years lost, and her voice is like yesterday."

"I remember your mother as well, with some fondness. Her cookies, mainly. Is she well?"

"You forget to whom you speak. I know nothing of my mother's health."

"You do not correspond?"

"My father is passed away."

"Oh…"

"You remember nothing of him, am I correct? Of course, no; for he drank and slept the days away, and not a soul ever saw him. The back room was his home, even as Mother entertained the children in the front. He died of yellow eyes, swollen belly. The smell of him was frightful, and afterward, Mother lost her senses. She never uttered a lucid word again."

Skeeter rests a hand at her back, feeling thin skin and bone vibrate as she speaks.

"Our home seized by creditors," she continues, "we moved south…or perhaps east."

"Which one?"

"It matters not. To Midland Township we traveled, to the charity of family."

"Midland, in the Louisiana Territory?"

"Yes, I suppose. We stayed with my uncle and my two cousins—older boys. The cousins began coming to me by night. I made no commotion, for they threatened to hurt my mother. Later I came to love those boys, the both. Silly girl I was, unable to keep myself pure, safe…from the loving of men, and from loving them in return. It seemed a natural thing, or perhaps foulest injustice. 'twas a wrong we shared as one—a shame for all to bear and none. Who is willing to claim it? Too many

65

optimists, blind, blind, silly people…"

Eyes gray-blue in the morning gloom, she gazes straight through him. "And you, O savior, where were you?"

Mother brings a tray and a delicious smell with her. Two cups of tea make lemon steam. Chunks of fresh bread are lightly burnt from the stove's flame, covered in butter and sugar-cinnamon. Skeeter gives her thanks and takes the tray eagerly. Mother disappears.

"Delicious," drones Luz. "Have you a beverage stronger than tea?"

He is confused for a moment as to her meaning. Then he hurries to the liquor cabinet beneath the family photos, returning with an unopened bottle covered in dust. She reads the label and sighs, "This will do."

"My family barely drinks."

"Of course, perfect son." She cracks the seal, pours a bit of liquor in her tea, a bit more in her mouth. Her face shows improved demeanor.

"I enjoy the things you say," he tells her. "At times they make no sense, but still I understand."

"Hmm, well…I found eloquence a dismal study in University. So many rules and conventions. So many better pursuits in which to lose oneself…"

"You went to University…in Midland?"

"Of course; I was not a truant. I broke no law until later, unless you count the professors, taking favors. Talented student, they all agreed, giving me fine grades for barely any schoolwork. Many private office visits apparently sufficed." She laughs, bitter.

"How came you to these parts anew?"

"Troubles there, and I enjoy the climate here…in truth I know of no other places. I found Jonathan's ventures, and a good living. Silly man, he never recognized me. Even now, he does not know me, but for being one of his best girls."

"Brute."

"Savvy businessman, scrupulous to a fault."

Skeeter snorts. "Jonathan?"

"The same." She sighs, then becomes resolute, eyes strong upon him. "We disagree, but one matter must be clear between us: you shall never tell him my true name, nor anybody in this township—for troubles will multiply."

Skeeter is silent, aware of having broken her admonishment already.

She sips the tea, ignores the toast. Then, a miracle! Of all things, she commences to make pleasant conversation. "Your family, they are well? Your father..."

"Changeless," he says.

"You have a brother, much older. His name escapes me."

"Batiste—named for my father," Skeeter tells her. Then he realizes he has said the name aloud, an act avoided for years. He stares grimly.

"What? What happened?"

"Batiste..." He says the name again, pauses...and decides he will survive a telling of the story. "He perished, when I was twelve. Just twenty-two, scarcely out of University. He took a job at the grain refinery, a perilous place. The dust of grain floats in air, friendly to fire. A spark, and...seven mothers cried that day. I refused to believe the news. But when he never returned home...."

The sudden appearance of her face, withdrawn emotion, flat expression, reveals her passive style of empathy. She groans with the smallest conviction.

"It was an odd time," he adds.

"An odd time? A bad time," she corrects, for she despises optimism.

"There lies the strangeness of it. Bad in anyone's eyes,

67

but to live it was simply odd."

He becomes distracted by the eddying movement of the
fog past his window. To be within the mist is to be within a
cloud resting on the earth—the nearest pleasure to the impossible
experience of flying through air. He is lost in the thought of it,
wondering what it might be like.

She nudges him roughly. "Is it within your plans to finish
what you are saying?"

He comes back, searches for grounding, and continues:
"Family life…after Batiste's death. Father worked harder than
ever, Mother became kinder than ever, quieter…aside from these
not a thing was changed. Not a routine was disrupted. I worry
that my own disappearance would make so scant a splash."

"'twas an awful splash, understated and unacknowledged"
she says flatly, cocoon around her passion. "I say your family
inhabits a blunted world. Asleep, all of you. Wake, wake, little
flower…"

She chuckles at her own words, against every desire to be
solemn.

He grins as well, surprised. Perhaps she understands;
perhaps she does not, but he feels compelled to tell her
everything.

"Orson believes that period began my decline," he says.
"I lost interest in…the various pleasures of life, some of which he
names essential. Many, I never had opportunity to discover,
being so young and having no more heart for excitement. He
cares all the less for me today; and I feel his wish, to revive the
Peter L'adorsity of old, that we would enjoy life together again."

"Orson," she interrupts. "I remember that little devil.
How is he?"

"Changeless, like Father, but opposite. Twenty-two, and
he refuses to mature."

"A trait you share with him?"

"Each in our own way, I suppose…"

A deep pulsating rumble emanates from the street outside the house. Its nature is initially a mystery, so unfamiliar is it. Luz recognizes the sound first, jumps up from the bed. "An automobile…"

They move to the drawing room, where the window looks forward. A vehicle is indeed at the front, idling at the roadside. The top is closed against the moisture of the day, and several men sit within. A large figure, hair of walnut, exits and stands searching. His hat and mosquito netting are off.

"Jonathan," Skeeter mumbles. "How did he know?"

"Where is my horse?"

"In the back yard."

"I will go home now…"

"No." He compels her gently back to the bedroom with the flat of his hand. "Stay here. I will see to Jonathan."

She rolls her eyes to signal sarcasm. "What pleasure, that brutish men come to violence on my account…"

Matthew

Daylight but a word, feeble against peaking mist that renders all things opaque, air like off-white linen; the city, neighborhood and grassy yard are swathed in it.

How many men are inside the car? Neither that, nor identities of any, are revealed; perhaps the brothers Turner, out en masse; perhaps others in Jonathan's employ. Skeeter closes the front door soft behind, as to shield his family's inner sanctum from the coming storm. Defiant face he wears, heart pumping fright he dare not feel. Toward keenness of senses, quickness of limb let it add, and never faintness of will. Even so, a quiet thought reminds him: "Your older brother lives no more to protect you..."

He marches forward toward the shadow, dark within white.

Jonathan stands mid-yard, wide-set boots sunken in grass

dewed as last eve. A pleasant face he wears, but a subtle scowl at the forehead betrays his tension.

"Young L'adorsity," he says, in that familiar tone, like a politician making a train stop. "I seem to have lost one of my ladies. Have you seen her?"

"Perhaps consult your source who sent you to me. If trustworthy, then take what you know on good account. If not, then for what reason shall I know the whereabouts of any lady?"

"I do have information that a certain Lauren is with you."

"Then trust what you know." Skeeter replies dismissively. "Having settled that, what remains with which I may assist you?"

Restrained coarseness of irritation enters into Jonathan's song. "Friend, do not feign I have no concerns here, for the lady is contracted with me. Perhaps you have a favor in mind, a natural thing for any man. If so, you need but ask; a day's pay is all you shall owe, at your current salary..."

"That I take hold of a woman with obtuse hand, casting off the joy of her as a dog leaves his mark forgotten on every fence—the value of this a day's pay? Where any man grasps not the value of what he buys, he surely pays exorbitant. Indeed, they ought pay nothing, those who perceive as little."

From Jonathan comes forced laughter. He steps back. "One does not consider the male urge as an item to be purchased and displayed proudly in the drawing room, but as a thing men shall pay well to be free of for a time. You see no value in that?"

"On the contrary, I see the highest value. Therefore I lay no hand upon any lady of yours, as what is priceless cannot be had for mere a day's pay."

"From any other, I would not accept this. But I believe you, and that is the funniest. Very well. Now send the woman out, that we may escort her home." He smiles, gray in the mist, and his breathing is quick with secreted ire.

"The lady is my guest, a courtesy of greater import than

71

any need you may have of her."

The other's face reddens. "Little mosquito, why are you a pest? I accepted you two nights ago by Orson's wiles, even as my own instincts begged halt—and now my fears are proven sound." He halves the distance between them. "Allow this animosity to rest. Send the woman out, as tribute toward peace between us."

And Skeeter halves it again. "So many ladies in your entourage…you will survive without this one," he says, bracing for the coming violence. "Go, therefore; do your business with gladness…"

"Memories of my past, you are there, flitting to and fro, that I be obliged to strike you away. Deliberate, willful, unjustifiable…" Jonathan's speech rises to a storm of curses, words nearly extinct in this enlightened age.

"Chivalry, Jonathan…"

A growl, and the first blow comes as on a schedule, for all this was foreseen. Skeeter's head clangs like a bell with the energy of it, hot blood runs from nose to mouth to chin, and he crumples to the grass, an empty sack.

In these fiercest of times, instants pass for hours. An eternity hangs hushed while Skeeter wins an internal war with vertigo. And, nearly the same instant, he is on his feet again. With a roar, he lunges at the larger man's midsection, ignoring poorly angled blows to his head and back. Jonathan reels backward, keeps sure footing until his heel finds a gopher hole; then he is off balance and down hard at the bottom, rolling with the speed and force of it. Ha! Skeeter, at the advantage, jumps to the middle of Jonathan's supine form. He lands a dozen savage hits to the other's face, pounding and pounding in a tense animal haze, blood mixing with blood.

Strong hands are at Skeeter's back, a brutal tug secures his hair, and he is lifted bodily up and confined. Car doors are open, the brothers now are loose, and the one who shrugs holds Skeeter's arms. Jonathan rises with a broken scowl and steps deep, giving full force to a blow at young L'adorsity's abdomen. Jonathan's brother Matthew appears from the misty void to land another, a joyous cackle at his lips. They are upon him one and all, without mercy, each punch adding pained emptiness to Skeeter's lungs. He gasps, choking at nothing.

"Enough," someone cries at last. Skeeter is released, to circle away unsteady.

"Lauren!" Jonathan shouts at the air with finality. And Luz comes, leading her saddled gelding 'round the house from the back. Jonathan eyes her crookedly through one good eye, cynical satisfaction showing on his bloodied face. "Or shall I call you...Luz?"

Luz recoils physically, as the day previous, then presses on with determination.

"Chivalry," Skeeter taunts, wiping his bloodied nose with a sleeve. "A contest of five to one, coward. I beat you..."

Jonathan ignores him, motions to the one who shrugs to take the horse. The brothers, energy spent, wander about, collecting hats fallen on the lawn.

"I beat you," Skeeter yells again, louder, that all the neighborhood hear. "Consult the bruises on your face if you doubt the history. Coward!"

"Quiet, you fool," says the one who shrugs.

Skeeter brushes past Jonathan leading Luz to the car. He takes her shoulders, leaving mud on her sleeves. "I will collect you at midnight," he whispers soft, that only she hears.

Her eyes are dull and pained both. Into the car she goes without a word, followed by the brothers. There is angry laughter from the men and the engine revs, the beast away down the street in little time. The one who shrugs remains, mounted upon Luz's horse. He looks sadly at Skeeter, then shrugs and trots away, following the departed automobile into the coalesced rumble of Moorhead. All is as it was; the entire business to naught...

Elsewhere in the distance a gray figure watches, nearly lost in the stubborn murk. Lanky and tall, the figure shifts and fidgets, trying to see without being seen.

Skeeter calls: "You there..."

At the sound, the figure skulks away, invisible in seconds, gone. A familiar walk, graceless tromping feet...

Orson.

Skeeter finds a bush, vomits blood and bile to the soil. All is shortness of breath and misery for a moment. Then he collects himself, finds his hat muddied and trodden. Shaken into shape, it fits well to tame his tousled hair.

Mother braves the outdoors at last, coming to her son with a towel. "You boys...will the fighting ever end?"

Skeeter takes the towel, holds it hard to his nose. Bleeding halted, he produces a painful smile for her. "This time," he says, "'tis important."

"Important, of course; else, who should bother with it? A toy one time, candy the next...today, a girl. The reasons change as ages, but the fight is forever..."

The talk already long for her taste, Mother kisses his yellowed-bruising cheek and prepares to walk inside. She cares not for the who-and-why of circumstance. Simply that her son has survived this day, is aware of her love; this is enough.

Then, perhaps as a favor to Father, she pauses and adds: "If such fire runs in your blood, ought you not follow Mr. Ladorsity's profession, as he so implores? With papers and reasoning, civilized battles are fought and won. The struggle no less, and the warrior within him shall ache for the sport of it 'till the day he dies..."

Skeeter makes not aloud his reply, for it would hurt his

mother. Verily he believes Father a humorless troll, ne'er to be emulated. Civilized battles? Are not battles without but distraction from battles within? Wars come as transients, loud and needy nuisances, and so we give them attention for a time. But when they at last release us to our peace, which restless soul shall seek more?

Mother departs to the indoors, leaving him alone in the uncaring mist.

He refuses, though, to remain beneath any ill spirit from the morning. Even now lives in him an unaccountable refreshing of energy, the various juices of fear and fight coursing about the body with nothing to attack. So he finds Orson's bicycle to set about remedying a broken drive chain. Fetching a few of Father's tools from the shed, he disassembles the confusing mechanics of the thing, discovers that the chain is not broken at all, but merely off the gear. A great many experiments later he comes away, fingers black with grease and, behold! The machine is good as new.

The somber day now promises to clear in increments; a shade or two lighter it appears already. He debates riding the bicycle into Moorhead to see Elder Krauss, for there summons now a kinship with that strange charlatan—of old, as though it has always been. Or perhaps young L'adorsity suffers merely the lack of any other trustworthy soul to consult, want for any activity to busy his mind 'tween now and dark.

To the township, yes, he decides—but enough of that cunning contraption. The time has come to return to his accustomed ways, for a man lacking patience to walk simply lacks patience.

He enters the house to clean up face and body filthy from the brawl. Donning fresh clothes in his room, he pauses to stare at the spot on his bed where Luz spent the night, wrinkles on the sheet still telling the shape of her. An ache crushes upon him, mysterious nostalgia for her presence. The best moments they were not, but to have them back now…certainly would tide this new void within him.

All is different today. It feels less than right to his independent spirit—such intense focus upon another, such hopeless girl and her whereabouts. Has she resumed the foul routines of her work, even now?

He wonders long, wonders more, and wonders why he wonders.

With a sigh, he returns the liquor bottle to the cabinet, the tray of toast crumbs to the kitchen. All things to their rightful place. Presently it is time to take Orson's trusty machine for one last ride to its master's house.

On the way he delivers Father's breakfast, now an early lunch and lukewarm besides. The basket fights the bicycle all the distance to the office, refusing to perch between the handlebars or hang peaceably at the side. The wicker strap sits sturdy between clenched teeth, however, so he makes good speed along the street, appearing a madman with the bulky thing suspended at the chest, grinning like an angry dog.

Within the smoky workplace, 'tis fortunate that Father never raises eyes to look upon his son, for the bruises are full up now, blue and raspberry-red half-circles beneath each eye, a swollen cheek and lip. The deposit is made with haste, and none but perfunctory greetings.

Quick thereafter comes the arrival at Orson's where, mercifully, the curtains to the room are closed. No confrontation shall occur today, much as Dear Reader may wish to eavesdrop. These young friends lack bravery even to speak with such malice preordained, such confused feelings—squirmy and cross and sad all the same—between them. Instead, Skeeter dismounts and leaves the bicycle exactly where he found it one day previous.

Like a benevolent thief, he departs with silence unbroken.

The sky, white as he crosses the river, evolves nearly to blue at his reaching the downtown.

That tiny storefront chapel should easily be lost in the great township, so alike are any two byways. But owing to healthy bearings and a ration of good fortune, young L'adorsity stumbles upon it at the first attempt.

Where Krauss stood yesterday: only bare sidewalk today. And, of all things, the door is locked!

Skeeter taps, peers into opaqued windows...to no success. The exterior of the establishment looms indifferent. He stands squinting in the sun. Perhaps the encounter of yesterday was with a ghost or an angel. Skeeter believes in neither—indeed, if Krauss be an angel, an inept one is certain, for all the new troubles mounted since their first meeting.

Young L'adorsity—as is his propensity—allows his musing to be broken, this time by a particular couple passing nearby, a young man and woman. Coworkers on a break, he assumes, for they look to be headed for the nearby café. Much is clear from the way they hold themselves: the woman enjoys the man's attentions—or perhaps there is no better diversion available—but she wants no illusions as to them ever being lovers. As for the man, he is unreadable, keeping all paths open.

Typical...

The two reach the end of the block and abruptly change course, disappearing 'round the corner.

At the thought of the café, a new idea arises, mental vision of dumplings and tea, complete with recollected smells. It is tempting, even with his sore stomach—and as further incentive, three dollars remain in his pocket.

Then again, no; there are priorities. He came here to find

Krauss. Therefore a walk about the block locates an alley, and the dusty rears of the storefronts. Skeeter counts doors, looking to locate the chapel's counterpart.

There in the lee of the alley—utterly unexpected—he comes upon the same couple again. Now they lean as one against the brick edifice, in the midst of a kiss—passion like a long-held strain of orchestral tension. They notice nothing of him, and they distract him again, even without intention, for he finds their lack of distraction…amusing. Further, he is amazed at his earlier failure of discernment: not merely coworkers, but secret lovers?

Then again, while these so skillful are rarely found out by others, ever do they claim a worse fate—they are found out all the same every moment their own consciousness should endure, the self being the strictest judge and keenest deceiver rolled into one. A taffied mess must be their minds.

The world brims with lovely things. To earn them is easy, to accept natural—but to take? To wrest from life's grasp something more? It seems unscrupulous, in the face of all that is given by air, light and Providence. He does not envy them their lot.

Yet a trace of something, perhaps the same shade as envy, does ache within. To his mind springs the girl in Orson's bed, that moment of similar feelings—of exposure to matters disallowed. These troubled thoughts must be inevitable for one of his persuasion—the mind of a man paired, as it is, with the heart of a boy.

It makes him unwell; something within him calls loudly for change—even a precursor would suffice. But how does one change his own heart, to become un-stunted?

The solution, perhaps, is to follow the lead of these alley lovers, taking more than is granted—even polite. Last night was a beginning, perhaps the first unwise act of his life, and simultaneously his first instinctive step toward joining the company of men. For he saw and took what he wanted, leaving innocent passivity behind.

Jonathan came and took her back, granted, but this too can be undone.

He told Luz to prepare at midnight tonight. Prepare for what? He well knows, or perhaps he has not decided—the intent matters little until the act is taken.

Thus, a plan for this eve now quietly forms in the darker regions of young L'adorsity's mind. Inspiration comes where it may; and all inspiration is potent toward great or awful end.

Presently a feeling of trespass—even in this public alley—reminds him to look away from the couple, lest they awake and find him staring. He resumes the hunt for the back door of Krauss' chapel, to trespass within and to safety. He finds a likely candidate and pulls.

Thankfully the door opens quietly, and a darkened interior shows. He slips through, closes the door behind, that the alley's influence at last be ended. Then he calls in a hushed voice: "Elder Krauss…"

His previous concerns are vanished quickly.

From within the dark does come the strangest music he has ever perceived.

Krauss

A tiny passage bent to an L steers to the main church area, sufficient to hold a half dozen benches—not pews. The floor is bare wood, but for a strip of carpet leading to a hand-fashioned pulpit, unmanned at the moment. The place broods abandoned, yet queerly holds a sacrosanct energy, like static of a lightning storm. No electric fixtures are seen; a dozen candles burn futile against the gloom.

And there stands Elder Krauss, back turned, assiduously whitewashing the east wall of the rented space with but a large brush. As entertainment perhaps, loudly does the man sing a tune—alas tuneless for lack of proficiency. Arcane lyrics echo about the vaulted chamber, bearing meanings ambiguous as their tonality—perhaps composed in a mix of the Sioux language and the immigrant tongue. Of the stanzas Skeeter can discern, many seem directed at him, as though the charlatan perpetually seeks to predict the future...

O desperate gaze, of wants unmet
Unsettled mind, most dogged set
In blight of blindness, hard of heart
Let every troubled youth depart

Sensing the presence in the room, Krauss turns, squints, and a grin sprouts among the whiskers.

"You. I know your name. Yet I fear I've forgotten the first and second half..."

"L'adorsity..."

"Ah yes, the mosquito," Krauss replies, voice at its customary muted timbre. "Scourge of the plains. I detest the name, not merely for the poor eloquence accomplished in uttering a word so patently colloquial. I object to the image it evokes. For every man from time to time shall be pest to another—a most joyous calling it is, righteous persecutors that we are. Teachers, correctors one and all."

"Indeed, I have been a pest today."

"But who shall follow the analogy so far as to dine on human blood? This is not in you; therefore, let us dispense with the alter ego...Peter." Krauss sets down his brush and approaches for a greeting, hands spotted in paint. "How are you today?"

Young L'adorsity grins back, the move causing him pain. He begins with small talk, as an honest reply to the question would be inelegant. "Apologies, for my entry by the back. The main door is locked..."

"Locked? Oh, my mistake. Still, it appears, those who seek verily to enter manage to do so in spite of hardship." Krauss moves closer, curious. Light falls upon Skeeter's battered features, and the other whistles in amazement. "A new look, I

81

see. The latest style is facial bludgeoning?"

"Indeed, popular with the young people."

"Good to stay in fashion, I agree." Still closer the other man draws, until he is near enough to grasp hands with Skeeter, but he waits. "This brings to mind my question of you yesterday…"

"I remember all but the first and second half. What was the question?

"…have you decided what troubles you?"

Skeeter's turn to chuckle. "I had not to decide, for a trouble chose me."

"A multitude, it appears…" At last Krauss clasps hands for a time, that understanding may come. And he says, "I do not understand this…"

"I, as little…"

"Well," Krauss continues. "A beating such as you've taken—invariably it be endured in favor of money or a woman. You are not the greedy sort, I suspect; therefore I implore that, however enticing said female is, you shall give no thought to pursuing her any further."

"I am not pursuing the woman. I have befriended…"

"Befriended? No man suffers danger for friendship's sake. Verily, love is the culprit.

"A new friend, and an old friend, all in one…"

Krauss sighs. "You shall need to tell a long story, as these hints impart but confusion. Have you the time?"

"I have none but time; and you?"

"'tis my calling," Krauss replies. "But, an honest query first: Are you so willing to help a poor soul who smells, alas, not as sweet as this woman you would assist?"

Skeeter waits, unsure…

Krauss motions at the painting job. "Lend a hand, and I will hear your story…"

"Oh…" Skeeter sighs. The wall before him appears vast, whitewash having been applied only to a small portion. Krauss laughs and searches about, by and by locating another brush in fair condition. He opens a second can of the mordant fluid and they take a region each of them, spreading pure white over the dingy surface in side-to-side strokes.

Meantime Skeeter recounts the events of the past day and night, of discretion omitting references to prostitution, fainting and kidnapping. A disjointed, baffling tale it is; Krauss grunts confusion all through the telling. Therefore Skeeter is obliged to retell the story with baser facts included. This time Krauss simply chuckles and nods, and all the while the regions of white expand upon the wall.

Eventually, the Elder chooses time to pause. He balances the brush at the brim of his can, pulls an old smoker's pipe from a shirt pocket. The brush hangs steady a moment, then tips into the paint with a gurgled splash. He groans, fishes it out with two outstretched fingers, still holding the unlit pipe in his other hand. At last, problem resolved, he stands and crosses to Skeeter's end, striking a match against an unpainted portion of the wall. The smell of rich tobacco fills the room, more mild than Father's.

"I would inquire first," Krauss begins, "as to the source of your current passions. Is it concern for the girl, or rivalry with this old enemy, Jonathan? Love and hate, they are of the same hue in the dark—light a candle, that you may see which one troubles. Perhaps you love Jonathan and hate Luz. Perhaps you love them both…"

Skeeter checks the other's face for joking—the face is serious. "Jonathan is the problem," he reminds him.

"Young L'adorsity, you may carve your world into archetypes of good and evil, but old Krauss perceives no such dichotomy. Simply shades of all sorts in each of us. Assume not to divine truth; only find heroism or error in your own acts. Is not what happened this day, of a part, your doing?"

"Perhaps, but ever more did fate force my hand."

"Fate? Took you no glee in goading poor Jonathan, that changeless lout? Ha! You plucked him, as a musician coaxes sound of a lute, the outcome as predictable. Who shall blame an instrument for the music emanates from within, as purposed?"

Skeeter's silence is faintly sullen, at a reprimand even gentle as this.

He breaks from painting, unlocks the front entrance and opens it wide. The shades at the large windows are easily pulled aside as well, and the small increase in illumination dwarfs the feeble candles. Now the fresh whitewash looks uneven, all imperfections exposed. "We shall need a second coat," he concludes.

"Give it time to cure." Krauss responds easily, still puffing his pipe.

Skeeter resumes painting, reaching within for a motive to continue their talk. This Krauss is a puzzle, yet he behaves as one who knows—a thing or two at least—likewise with joyful zeal in the knowing. Has any other friend such a gift?

For all his deliberate confidence, Skeeter of late inhabits a strange new place of unknowing. Alongside thoughts of vengeance, he feels the tugging for some essence of certainty. Therefore, to collect crumbs from a wise man's feast, like a dog scuttles 'round the family table, this be an apt ambition for today.

As for his other intents, they will wait for tonight.

"Now here is a puzzle," Krauss continues. "Yesterday I met a man who claimed to be happy, and today you come complaining of all misfortune—I would be tempted to count all my predictions validated. But from where I stand, this is not the case; your countenance today appears much more purposed and alive—facial damage notwithstanding. In relative terms, yesterday you were a sleepy ghost, content in static afterlife.

Now I wonder…what has occurred that you are so awake? Is indignation such a stimulant?"

Skeeter ponders. "Something in Luz: a dazzling energy."

"But as you tell it, she craves nothing but self-pity and alcohol. What inspiration find you in such a being?"

"A bitter sense of humor. A warmth seldom seen, the challenge of calling it forth…"

"I hear you searching and not finding. Listen, Peter: Energy is perceived where differences exist, as between what is and what was, the algebraic sum being what has been lost. Therein lies the commonality of you and her." Krauss appears satisfied a moment. Then, seeing the other's puzzlement, he rouses and comes close, smoke following him. "What is lost to you, dear friend? What is lost, that you are so stirred by the sadness in another?"

Skeeter smiles politely for no other face to make. "So many questions…where shall I begin to answer a one? And what has any of this to do with mathematics?"

Krauss chuckles, ignores him. "I told you yesterday, I was a messenger as a young man. This was rewarding, but eventually I tired of delivering messages of others. I left my life, left the township entirely, and traveled to Sioux country, where I studied whatever aroused my interest. And I met a wife—lovely woman, wise and majestic creature. I was content. I was one with the land, one with the sky, and one with her."

He pauses to refill his pipe, watching as Skeeter continues to paint. "A fine job," the Elder remarks. "Perhaps a bit more paint on the brush."

"I am nearly finished, and I have completed the bulk of it singlehandedly…"

"'tis your choice, young Sir. Your diligence is appreciated." Krauss lights, puffs, and continues his story: "One day, my life changed. A fire. My wife was killed."

85

Skeeter stops painting, stunned. Compassion turns sharp and discordant, like a knife directed at oneself.

But Krauss' face is a paradox, appearing not pained in the least.

"With me mourned all the community," the Elder continues, "immigrant and native alike. All their support mattered little, for I became bitter. Anger pure as this shall not be confined, but shall spread reckless and selfish unto all things. Life itself, humankind, Providence, all these drew my rage. My vocabulary shrank to none but destruction. In the end, I had no heart to hurt another, little cruelty to lash out at my friends. Therefore I became a polite corpse, walking, talking, breathing…death and life as one.

"And ever did my wife haunt me still, but her ghost was not her spirit; 'twas merely my sadness with her likeness attached…my own creation entirely. And so I was obliged to cast her memory far from me, to be free of it. I denied all that she had ever been."

The elder taps young L'adorsity on the arm, that he turn, for he has resumed painting. "That—not her death—was my greatest loss, and so unnecessary," he concludes.

"Why unnecessary?"

"I assumed my actions would heal me, but I was wrong. All my efforts merely created a lingering ruin. I saw this truth at last; and when I saw it, I released myself. I released my wife's memory. I released Providence, and I was healed."

"Healed? I cannot believe this…"

"Look upon me. See you a scar upon my being? Feel you a motive impure within me?"

Young L'adorsity cannot deny the point, for his senses absorb the man's peace. "How? How is this accomplished?"

"I shall not tell you, as my answer is of little meaning. Only your answer will be for you to hear, in that time you are prepared to speak it."

"Riddles. What sort of messenger tells all and stops at a solution?"

"An honest one. I simply help you see your need. You do well enough as you are, but you need a new way…"

"My father is your age," Skeeter tells him. "And in my house, no wisdom is found. How can this be? Why am I cursed to be raised by such a man?"

"It simply is. Again, your place is not to mourn the error seen in others, but only to bolster or correct your own acts. Your father's faults, do you see them in you?"

"Never."

"Deny the inevitable, and you lose already. See your enemy coming—then you have a chance to parry. Perhaps you should pursue the woman after all, since she has disturbed you so skillfully. Only true love has this power, to infuriate…"

"Indeed?"

"Verily, to pursue her will be difficult; do you understand this? To grant good to a person who believes in nothing is…impossible in most cases."

"I am good…"

"Are you? All believe in their own goodness, and most are mistaken. But if it be as you say, she will see it—unless she kills you first. I am joking. Look, you are almost finished with the wall!"

"True." A few more strokes, and Skeeter sets down his brush with satisfaction. "'twas easy, with so much help from you…"

"There is the west wall…" Krauss indicates the far end of the chapel, still ugly with the color of dirty socks. "I have more paint, if you have stories…"

"Have you no parishioners for these labors?"

"I shall need to stand in the front again tomorrow, it

appears. 'tis my calling, whatever its success." Meantime the Elder acquiesces to the hint, and begins stowing the paint cans. "Have you learned enough then?"

Young L'adorsity moves toward the door, at the last calling back: "You have taught me that my instinct is trustworthy; that I shall indeed make my way back to the company of men. Therefore, I leave you with sorrow, for we will not meet again."

"Oh? What will you do?"

"Tonight, I abscond from this place, this corrupt township. And, though you be not pleased, I must confess in advance of my wrongdoing. This very eve, clothing myself in all stealth, I shall steal Jonathan's prize mare…"

Mare

The house is dark, but for the largest window at the front. The parlor: candles flicker, figures move. Laughter, voices, and cigar smoke seep unevenly to the outer airs. Perhaps Jonathan tells a boastful story even now, each wave of his hand tossing ale from glass to floor with drunken obliviousness. These sights and sounds are typical of the Turner home at evening's peak. Brothers and friends here gather to celebrate the passing of time, one day nearer sweet demise, for what more occasion has a barren soul to mark? No day stands apart from any other, but for the weather—which has turned sullen. Whatever moon may smirk above is cowed by dull clouds, the threat of precipitation leaving scent of electric tension in the air.

Skeeter slinks like a night creature, advancing via a stand of bushes at the limit of the property. Here he leaves his backpack before making trespass on the grassy frontier. He pauses a moment to heave one piece of the jerky he brought—taken from the reserve in the L'adorsity kitchen—over the house. The first throw, uncannily accurate…he hears the jerky fall near the dog's house in the back yard. He cannot see the reaction, but the plan is for the animal to be pleased. Will it remain pleased when he intrudes upon its territory?

As it happens, the dog is less trouble than the goats. The carnivore is entirely docile, fierce protector turned lapdog by a little more meat and Skeeter's innate tranquil manner. The goats, lesser creatures, begin bleating immediately at his encroachment, and they will not stop. He must use a few of the apple slices—also brought from his kitchen, but for the horse.

The offering quiets the goats. Too late.

In the house, voices pause; heavy boot-steps make way for the rear door. Skeeter dives cover 'neath a feed trough just as the door creaks wide. An inquiring head peers into the dark of the yard, where animals fidget and one man holds his breath, even while thanking Providence for the obscured moon.

Long seconds pass.

The door closes, and the boots move back to the main room for more smoke and liquor. Fool! Too lazy even to fetch a torch.

'tis true: criminals hold a magical view of the world, and a blind faith in its blessed nature…that they may imagine full glory in ruining it. None foresee that the sheep may rise to slay the wolves one day. And so, in false security, the wiliest criminals this end of Moorhead do permit themselves to be robbed by the village idiot.

Jonathan's prize mare, what fine beast she is—tall, with sinewy muscles flowing at every graceful movement. Spirited as well, she jogs her head boldly as young L'adorsity approaches. He stands just beyond the corral, passing bites of the apple, gaining trust with practiced patience. After a time he opens the wood gate with care to avoid a creaking; finds Jonathan's saddle and fastens it 'round the animal's girth; slips the bridle past her ears with gentle touch. He mounts her and prepares to guide her past the house.

Footsteps again, and many this time. The back door bursts open and Skeeter molds his body flush to the mare's back, barely a shadow hiding him. If anyone has a torch to shine, all is lost.

The frightful moment calls back memories of a brutal beating just today. How severe might their wrath be if they find him here on their land, in the midst of a crime? Drunken and justified, they will be unstoppable. Perhaps he will not survive.

Matthew and another man linger at the back step, brandishing no torch as yet. It appears a dispute has arisen; intemperate voices banter artlessly, threatening severest violence at one another. But the talk goes long; soon it is clear that none intend more than to yell insults. By and by the mare is restless from the inert weight atop her; she rocks and fidgets. One of the men peers in Skeeter's direction, seeming to lock eyes. But it is illusion, thankful, for the dull-sighted brute sees but animals in the yard, noticing not even the corral gate ajar. The craftiest animal remains undetected.

Jonathan comes, and with strong hands pulls his young brother bodily indoors. All laugh and return in; the door slams the yard to silence.

Even over the tension of the moment, the brotherly gesture recalls better times in Skeeter's past. Oh to be outmatched by a sibling, to be corrected. Even to be bullied. Though a sour feeling at the time, he would return to it gladly now, if by magic it were possible.

Any brother shall be an improvement over a dead brother.

He decides that now is the time to make his escape. He strokes the mane hard, to calm the animal, then coaxes her forward. The gentle falls of hooves in soft dirt seem as deafening thumps in the cricketed stillness. Past the goats, the lolling dog, around the house and to the front he survives, picking up speed, keeping to the quieter grass and, behold! He is off the property. His deep breath exhales of its own doing.

At the bushes he swings low, nearly out of the saddle, to pick up the backpack left. As a reflex, a sudden fright, he urges the beast to full gallop on the shoulder of the road, so urgent is he to be away from the place.

Then at the coming calm, he feels every emotion held frozen by earlier fears. Thrill…and the laughter bubbles forth, boastful, with none to hear but the loping mare.

Guilt as well…

Now do not imagine, Dear Reader, that young L'adorsity feels remorse at this last act, of vengeance and rivalry born, for such deeds ring as justice to the fiery heart of the moment. No, another theft weighs heavy, committed but a quarter-hour prior.

Father L'adorsity, rogue that he is, keeps the balance of his earnings far from family, at the office. Here is where the good son commits his minor crime.

At this hour no cigar cloud looms; the man is at home, resting for tomorrow's exploits. The building is shadowed, the big desk vacant. Raised from a child around the place, Skeeter knows every opening, every trusty hiding hole. In via the roof, the still-warm attic space, and he drops to the floor through the ceiling flap, searching, locating Father's secrets within minutes. Rolls of money, enough for three of Jonathan's petrol-burning leviathans, packed in the lost space between two file drawers: all this and a family of modest comforts! A prudent inclination perhaps, saving for their future…or is the man merely hoarding?

Skeeter takes two hundred, leaving the rest for Father's reserves, doubting the loss will be counted. This is before the raid at Jonathan's house, and the money rides snugly in the pack bouncing at his back.

Still another guilt tugs at him, another act, committed prior to the raid at Father's office. Of poor manners essentially...the matter of leaving without a proper goodbye.

The note he composed is eloquent, as expected in any fine society. Yet, how can scripted word suffice for Mother's embrace, Father's last grudging look? An empty act it is, therefore, and heavy it hangs, like a weight inside young L'adorsity's chest. Left in his room at his leaving, the note reads:

> *Dearest family of my birth, place of my growing; from babe to man I make all my years in you, my world and universe. To Mother and Father, I do owe life and soul, shaped as I am by loving example and countenance, words of hope and correction, even the simple presence of you, ever and always. Love and goodbyes I convey this day, for my eye envisions another place, where life evolves yet without fine shelter and pardon, where I am free to succeed and fail by merit and choice alone. Faces of yours, ever etched upon memory's window; your voices shall be with me for all time. Your son, Peter.*

As for Grandmother, goodbyes are simple—a long look until she meets his eyes. Partial recognition...she knows from his face what is coming. No promise is kept forever; merely the attempt is heroic. The old woman smiles and looks away, dismissing him with no affront.

He slows the mare to an easy walk. For stealth's sake, he avoids Moorhead proper, taking a circuitous route around the township. 'tis nearly midnight when the plain two-story house bobs into being, a forbidding slate gray presence this eve.

'tis a night of many fears indeed, some past and more to

come. Skeeter knows not if Jonathan has stationed friends nearby the house, waiting to intercept any who approach. He knows as little of what Luz has confessed; perhaps she repeated his last whispered instruction to the laughing carload of his enemies. That she would betray him without qualm seems possible, for never has she shown more than casual interest in anything of him.

Mere faith draws him forward—that, and a new-found breakneck irreverence at all authority of rationality. Perhaps one and the same are these things.

Upon approaching her door, he learns quickly that, whatever her previous attitude, indifference is fled.

"You have ruined me," she announces immediately. "You come as a curse, in all the subtle ways destroying by mere touch…" The anger about her passive form looks somehow wrong, like a thing borrowed and not owned.

He dismounts the horse at the awning before her house, for she has come outside. Hat off, he stands taking in the sight of her.

"Who did you tell?" she demands.

"I told no one. But I discussed you…old memories of you, with Orson. He inferred much."

"Orson, that dolt. He came here midday, looking for a favor…he had already told Jonathan, of course. Now everybody knows my true name."

"Orson came here? You didn't…"

"Of course not, you fool. And Jonathan's face…a terrible thing you did to him." A reminding glance at Skeeter's bruises, and she adds: "He to you, as well. A silly, silly affair altogether."

Skeeter defers the outrage he would voice; simply raises a hand to stop her. "We shall not agree on all points. And I regret…I apologize for what has happened."

She is silent.

"Now I tell you this. Tonight, my time here is finished. I am leaving and I shall not return. I shall leave without you...or with you."

She notices the mare, glistening beside him. "Is that...Jonathan's horse?"

"It seemed fitting," he says, stifling a grin. "He needs her little now, with the new automobile."

"Fitting, yes," she says, trying to rally sarcasm, sounding no more than weary. "You would rob the man of all his females this eve?"

"I took the man's horse, yes, but you are none his property to be stolen. Further, I daresay he cherishes you less."

"That Jonathan cares little for me is not the point. With us there is business."

"I cherish you more...than anybody in this township, anybody in the world. I will protect you, I swear, to the last breath of life I possess."

"Words of a young soul. You love but the idea of me."

"Let me know you, that I may love this person as well. Travel with me tonight, for in this place of our birth, we are both lost."

She would have a clever answer; indeed, she tries to retort, yet somehow the argument is ended. A long and perfect silence, eyes met. Finally, she says simply: "The weather looks unkind. Sit with me inside, that I may dissuade you..."

"I am fearful every second I stand here. When the brothers find the mare missing, where, suppose you, will they go first?"

"Your house. They will not harm your parents?"

"Jonathan's father and mine are close friends...no danger of that. Yet upon realizing I am not home, you understand where they will search next."

She nods. "I see. We must leave immediately."

His face remains calm, yet he is bursting with elation not felt in years, for she used the word *we*. His purpose, uncertain until now, has been realized.

The same moment, a single drop of rain spatters his left cheek, like the first tear of a mother for a lost son. Another comes, and then another; soon a steady rain is falling, sufficient to mourn all the sons that ever were.

"We cannot travel in the rain," she says.

"I know a place nearby, shelter until the weather clears."

She packs quickly, a few clothes, soaps and medicinals. The whiskey is the heaviest item in her bag. Meantime he saddles her horse; and then they mount and ride, leaving her room open, candles burning. He directs her toward the southwest of the township, where the farms are large and intermixed with green-swathed herd lands.

"What sort of place is this, which you say you know?"

"There is a field where I believe the master of the farm tends not to duties. Perhaps he likes his liquor, for he leaves his cattle to wander all night. We may hide with safety in his barn, for he shall not be along to check it at this hour."

As to hurry them along, steady rain escalates to a savage downpour.

Luz

Imagine night.

Troubled night. Violent slabs of thunder rampage across the stormy airs. Dark nearly opaque, sodden grass gray and black, pounded nearly flat 'neath cruel attack of rain like blades. The wide meadow suffers in waves.

Meadow and sky are two, and in the meadow two riders pick and choose paths carefully to avoid falling awash, for spontaneous rivulets have appeared with nowhere to run.

Oblong shapes loom nearby, the outbuildings of a farm, interiors of which promise dry and safety. The riders aim for these, nearly blundering into a gathering of desperate cattle.

"Look," Skeeter calls, over hissing water. "Help me drive the cattle toward the shelter."

"Why?" She is of ill temper, soaked to the bone.

"Have you ever seen a cow with fever? Such misery I do

not wish on any creature."

She glowers, but complies. They separate, taking adjacent corners of the herd, perhaps fifteen head in all. Dancing to and fro with the horses, they succeed in annoying the cattle more than the rain; the group begins to move en masse toward the buildings. Skeeter coordinates the operation with shouted instructions, forgetting for a time the need for quiet. By and by a roofed corral seeps into proximity, other cattle enjoying relative dryness under its shelter. Now the cattle being guided recognize the familiar and begin moving toward it freely. With no small satisfaction do the riders watch the procession, for a tedious task it has been.

Rescue complete, Luz remarks smartly: "If your farmer sleeps through all the noise you've created, I should like to see his liquor cabinet."

"I shall buy you a liquor cabinet someday, and a farm in which to keep it."

"I shall expect it, for all my labors. The cabinet, not the farm, for I know nothing of the latter."

"What exactly do you know, my dear lady?"

"Nothing, save one, as I have said repeatedly."

They search the premises for an empty building. A barn their best hope, they are surprised at finding a small guest house, perhaps for hired hands. It is empty, and mattresses of a reasonable condition are within.

"Perfect," he notes. For modesty's sake they dry themselves and change clothes in the dark. They search for a candle and find an electric light instead. He hangs wet clothes to dry over the hot bulb, which eases the bone-white glow of the thing as well. At the windowless security of the room, Luz' temper improves. They relax, sharing a mattress. He leaves a hand at her back to feel her voice vibration.

"I put no trust in any human being, as a rule," she says.

"Now I have risked trusting you, of all people. Therefore I must know… Where shall we go? Have you the faintest thought?

"Of course, yes," he says. "When morning comes, with clear weather—let us hope—we shall continue south along the river, toward the dark hills. A trail is there, made wide by many who have taken it west. I mean to take you into the Wyoming lands, where the Sioux still roam free."

"Sioux? There are so many here in Moorhead; I see no reason to search for more of them. And I comprehend little of this talk of south and west. I simply ask directions when lost."

"To travel south, ride with the morning sun at your left. And to go west, ride into the setting sun." He sits up, excited with anticipation. "After we make our living with the Sioux for a time, perhaps we might move further west, for I have always wanted to see Mexico. San Francisco…a fine township as I have heard."

"Dear, I know nothing of these places. I do not want to go to Mexico."

He sighs. "What would you have then?"

She ponders, a long time; for perhaps she has never thought to give an honest answer to any question—so much work in it. At last she says, "I know not."

"I believe this," he says gently. "Therefore, let us go as far as Sioux country, and then decide what next. A trusted friend told me it is a good land, with help for what ails us, you and I."

"What ails us?"

"Does nothing ail you?"

"All does ail me, and nothing can be cured."

"All is curable. Life is good, fair fortune woven into her, innate…if a trifle elusive."

"Life is not good…"

"You are good," he tells her. "As nobility woven soul-deep. Believe this first, that you see it after; but by your touch I

99

know…I have felt it, always."

Luz rises to fetch the whiskey in her bag. She returns to sit, takes a swig from the bottle. "I am an unpleasant companion," she says. "Some days I do not leave my bed unless work forces me to wake. Every third day, at the least, I drink to a stupor…"

She sighs. He waits.

"You must tell the truth," she says. "Be not a dreamer at my expense. All these facts cannot be acceptable to you."

He takes the bottle, feels the weight of it, reflecting. "True, I do not share your affection for this."

She continues: "All hardships will come with time if we remain together. Evenings, when you have your stories with friends, you will celebrate your past…and what shall I celebrate? All my years are a secret void; I am born this day intact, shame indwelling for reasons long hidden; I am but a visitor wherever I am."

"You have not noticed? I am a visitor here as well. This much we share in common." He hands her the bottle absently, words fighting to take form at his lips: "But, of your past, yes, I am troubled to think even of today…the days previous frighten me still more…"

"I have lain with Jonathan," she adds, as to banish the subject before its inevitable arising. "A part of the employment process in my field. Long ago, of course…"

"Dear me, that is appalling." He pauses, long, but rouses and continues. "It matters not. You exasperate me in so many other ways as well. Strangest, I believe this fact has a part in my feeling alive, today as never before. Where a life without you would eliminate my current troubles, my flame would be extinguished as well. You are a problem I crave beyond tranquility. Let peace fall away, if turmoil be you."

"Silly, you make no sense…" Her comment is typical,

but a look of bland curiosity threatens to lift her features.

"By my eccentricity," he explains, "I am shielded from life. I am both special…and perhaps terribly ill. My interest is in all things equal—great and trivial alike—and by this my interest is in nothing. But in you I see a quality I lost in my mourning, that spirit of my youth—oh that you see your own innocence somewhere in me, and find…find one instant of clarity, even in this time of life and after all that has been broken. Oh that you see as I see, for verily this—straight through to your soul, dear lady, you are perfectly and astoundingly beautiful! And I realize…at last I realize the reason I never gave myself to love. The reason is…my love was come and gone, for I have always loved…you."

She turns abruptly as driven aggressively by something; she pushes at him, lips against his—she would go straight through him were it possible. He gasps sudden and allows it, tasting sweet woman spit. The smell of her is perfume, rainwater and sweat. The velvet soft of her is utterly new, the heat—body to body even through their clothes—like joy distilled,

Then she crumples into the crook of his arm, head against his shoulder, as though sated by merely a kiss. Silence, for a perfect moment, and breathing in unison.

"I do not kiss," she says, collecting herself. "Whatever I may do, I avoid the lips…"

"Then we find something special already."

Reluctant to part from the world he has discovered, he pulls her bodily to him until she rests upon his lap, straddling him cross legged, their bodies impossibly melded as one. He kisses her again, a long, long moment. Then, conceding that respiration must occur, he remains forehead to forehead with her, breathing of her breath.

"I want more," he says softly, "if it be special as this."

"Perhaps I understand you, at last," she says.

"Let us hope."

"Would you have me now, then? Out of these clothes?"

"Now indeed... and all the powers of the heavens and the low creatures of the earth shall rejoice with us, at having found a good thing when we believed in none."

"I feel silly; I am a schoolgirl again, my palms clammy, my heart racing."

But she sighs, sad even still. And again comes one of her unaccountable mood changes, heroic in light of the previous moment. She wriggles free of him, squatting like a bird on the bed nearby.

"Is this truly special, as you describe?" she asks, forlorn. "I see in your eyes lust, as in any man at this singular moment we have reached."

"If you say wait, then we will wait; my passions shall be secondary to my conscience."

"Conscience, conscience...I am sure Jonathan agrees, missing his mare even now..."

"A different passion entirely," he says, but averts his eyes, aware that somehow words have betrayed him. "You see my pronouncements as self-serving babble..."

"I believe you are sincere as you can be—to what self-knowledge you may possess. You think yourself unique. So strenuous is your undertaking to be a gentleman, even to prove yourself exceptional among men. But who assumes I want a gentleman? If a thing be rare, am I to see its value and crave it of accord?"

"You hate all things equally," he jokes.

Anger shows at her brow. "You mock me already..."

"Do not make insult of humor, in which you possess a fine talent as well. You are unfair to me, for stubbornness' sake, denying the good you see before you."

"The good," she repeats. "The good..."

And she stands to pace, not forgetting the bottle. Holding the burdensome thing, she makes a grumbling circuit of the room before returning to face him. "The Luz of your mind is swayed by such reasoning. You forget the one here in this moment—always this will be your failing. For I am not what ought exist by your reckoning; I am that lowly pawn of men, inevitable product of prosperous and scrupled society—a base need, and I serve it, for I am a base individual. Why seek you change that, even giving your own future as payment to the task?"

"My future? 'tis nothing. For you, all my futures, all that I ever possess scarce will satisfy my wanting…to edify you with my love."

"I do not ask for…edification. Therefore save yourself and let me as I am."

He stares, words depleted for the moment.

"'twas a lovely kiss," she adds tiredly. "It means nothing. Let us rest, for morning brings long travel."

She unplugs the lamp rather than search for its toggle. She takes a mattress separate from his and flops sullen, pulling a sweater 'round for warmth. "Goodnight, Dear."

He mumbles the same, stunned by the turn of events.

The room is black. Confusion and boiling blood prove a poor recipe for sleep. He smells her, even from where she lies. He tastes her on his lips, and the memory of the kiss is overpowering.

She is a passive soul, he knows. He could have her still, simply by rising and taking his fill with gentlemanly persuasion; the act is nothing for her. But he lies still, refusing to hear the call of such corrupt voice. Perhaps she expects—or hopes—his honor will fail, for her instinct was sharp regarding his motives; he must best all men, even to spite her.

Something like anger taunts him—at her use of all available strength, toward ruining every moment which tries

103

valiantly to be magic. Certainly she is afraid…of submission to life's rewards; ever in control, fighting furious to remain master of all, every passing relation, every possibility. That most powerful word—no! She builds a fortress of it. Adding a trusty bottle of courage, these are sufficient for life's survival.

He says all these things in silence, for it shall do little benefit to voice them. Two days into their affair and an impasse reached; sex initiated and deferred; and now sleep be angry, as a husband and wife in quarrel? The speed of it is intense; days like years.

This, he surmises, makes fine disincentive for strong relations. Easier to seek the simple trustworthiness of the banal world, multitudes of unthinking gears in that great machine, each exercising simple duty with pure motive.

Pure motive, his first love: damaged now at the hand of this woman.

But still he envisions her face, unseen in the darkened room, air of peaceful sleep like a glow settled about her. She exists there in all truth—innocence to be distilled that he may drink her like a fine liquor. Already drunk, he has been, at the mere thought of it. He feels corrected by the realization; but he cannot stop, unable to change the want that beleaguers like a thirst.

By and by, he calms. The grumble of rain on the roof is a droning lullaby. Smells of the old mattress and sogginess all about are sufficient to overcome the previous scents, and he drifts…off to sleep…tedium of wakefulness…supplanted by visions of lips and warmth and supple flesh…the body of woman, archetype of pure maternal femininity.

Woman holds, comforts of her lap, single finger stroking his forehead, a lock of baby hair. Cooing softly, she breathes music for his living ear…

For every soul a wand'ring path
Wild stream of no design
No loyal chart or knowing map
To mark the cyclone's eye
For every heart a burden hangs
Of added year and years
For each of us a different key
To loose the healing tears

Meaningless, meaningless, yet in dreams these words are right, for sleep, unbroken well into the night.
And for dreams, illuminating dreams…

Batiste

The bad bells are ringing all around, claxons of fire engines, steam- and petrol-driven alike. Residents are swift afoot—racing not away, but toward the fire—buckets in hand, harried faces.

Hazy in the distance, a chalice of smoke hangs gray within blue, vertex telling its source, tower of pure flame, greedy tongues of orange and black and death. The building is far, but appears close for its awesome size—the grain refinery.

Mother is gone, run screaming toward the disaster. Young Skeeter waits, Grandmother's hand soft at his shoulder. The old woman stifles sobs, for she already knows the day's end by its beginning.

As for the twelve-year-old, he understands nothing, sweet December of his innocence at hand.

Hours like days...evening comes, and still they wait at the

*front porch—she in her rocking chair, he fidgeting busily at the
stone step. The awful pyre, forgotten by him for the time being,
consumes itself to a pallid glow, and citizens begin returning
home, faces grimy, buckets hanging from despondent hands.
Mother and Father are among them, staggering uneven, leaning
heavy upon each other. At the lawn they part. Mother addresses
her mother with silent eyes, shaking her head; the old woman
simply sighs, sad truth confirmed. Father, perhaps for the last
time, looks long upon the living son dawdling unproductively at
the step. Then The Bereaved One enters the house and finds the
couch. Here he sits, head in hands, indefinitely.*

*Mother sags next to Skeeter on the rigid stone; The last of
the rescuers have passed, claxons silent, and the crickets have
started their night's business, oblivious to the agonies of
humanity so close by.*

*"Where is Batiste?" Young Skeeter asks, suspecting, not
knowing; the weight of both crushes awareness from his child
mind.*

*"Your brother is out there somewhere," Mother says with
finality. "But we will not see him again."*

*"Where? Where out there?" He sees none but dark, a
perfect evening*

*"Listen to the night, son. To a lovely place your brother
has gone, to nature's simpler concerns. Listen... and you will
hear him, always."*

Silence rouses him, thunderous absence that it is. The
rain has stopped. More powerful is the stillness from within the
room, solitude a distinct presence of itself. Something is missing.

He sits up, knowing instantly; a glance merely confirms
the fact.

She is gone.

He races to the door, to the outside, where playful

moonlight peers through now-billowy night clouds. Eerie
luminescence shows one horse remaining at the outdoor shelter.
Subtle disturbance of earth, a set of tracks leads across the
meadow in a southerly direction, lost in the distance. With a
groan he turns to the inside of the room, where the glow reveals
her bag—and of course her bottle—absent.

For once he cares nothing for the joys around him—
sounds living in the space, the drip, drip of water from the roof,
like little footsteps all around. The small house creaks and
groans. Utterly fresh post-storm air wafts into the room, a
wakeful, hopeful chill. He hears not, feels not. The door slams
fiercely and he collapses to the bed, eyes mashed tight, seething
with something like fury.

Coward, he thinks at her.

Then he says it aloud: "Coward! Stupid girl…stupid
whore!" Fists slam of their own volition at the mattress.
Knuckles still smarting from Jonathan's face burn fresh red with
the impacts. In his mind the mattress is Jonathan, at his mercy
anew. Skeeter pounds fists ever harder, the room echoing with
his thrashing.

Then the mattress is Batiste, brotherly face black-and-
white, grainy as a photograph. If ever a man deserves to be
bludgeoned, 'tis this deserter, for leaving a young boy with but a
troll for guidance. The home where life began and thrived…it
shrank sickly in his absence. So ends life's enterprise—a family
learns well after one such blow, is wont ever again to bring futile
hopes amid the violence of chance.

He wishes violence at Luz herself, tiny body frail against
his might. But he cannot conjure her face; so short-known,
already it fades. Only the child remains, the child he never would
harm.

That child is gone.

He feels an awful thing well up from him. Like a sick

stomach, deep soul's nausea, it expels itself, hot tears burning agony, ripping. A wail in the silent room, mournful, shameful…his own voice disconnected from body, the honest sound.

He wants to die.

Pain chokes like a mindless beast. Breathing is a gasp, spasms uncontrollable. This body of emotion is pitiless.

Time passes, agonizing; and somehow, peace comes…in luminescence like the moonlight. All around is eerie bright. The pain eases; he relaxes, catches breath, and then cries again, but as himself. In truth is expelled all that is foul; marvelous soul which heals itself needs no greater intercession.

He is silent, limbs fallen heavy at his side, stillness like a blanket wrapped snug. Points of space as one, time a weighty stone.

In a dream and a fog, a figure emerges. Young, blond; his own face smiles at him, real as life, clearer than memory. The eyes—they describe all the hues of bliss, golden timbre of joy. Lips muted, for superfluity of words; eyes speak sufficient. Sound of sight, language of ghostly inkling, gossamer weight of beauty pure, all is said, and sure.

"Batiste," he breathes.

The glow is dismissed; L'adorsity opens eyes to the ceiling, gloomy solid above, surroundings silent and real. Visions, like moments, pass away, mixed in memory with the mundane.

He sits up.

At his return to consciousness, revived intellect turns busy. Somewhere, someone begins asking why—why the weeping? Why the pain? It is not the woman, any more than catalyst be reaction. A deeper madness has afflicted, one that wore like life's heavy wool—indeed, 'twas composed of life's substance—but all the same a lasting dream, affable nightmare, world of all dimensions save consciousness. One only sees lesser light in hindsight. Wisdom of age as folly to a child, never are coming states foreseen with clear grasp.

"How long have I been away?"

An elated determination takes him by the hand, wanting to lead him to a new home; but this, being of the genuine sort, is unfamiliar. "Awake, you," it says. "And live! Life is good—is not that what you say?"

"My brother is dead."

"Truth."

"My family cares so little…"

"No! They are…overwhelmed."

"I am to blame, for thinking them gods?"

"Who has experience? Who is trained to exist of no volition, to live and grow and love and lose and mourn and be beaten, utterly beaten, by mere happenstance? Brightness and gloom—who, trained in one, has heart quick for the other? Who can change faces? Who knows, verily, what is to be done?"

Clarity attacks him, sigh of freshest air entering his lungs—even his own grievous errors come exposed. The realization brings a gasp of fright, that never would he have entered the company of men by stealth or force. Such company is not of men, but of beasts.

Evil as Jonathan may be, the evil is his—unless L'adorsity should take up same in the other's honor. To hate is to envy that which is hated, to attempt comprehension of that which infuriates; for men are curious creatures. In such perverse embrace are hate and love linked; one becomes the other soon enough.

For one smallish man to seek war against Moorhead's gangster elite, even calling it gallantry—what line is imagined between hero and foe?

In his way of seclusion—born of apathy, truth be told—he

comprehends little what a normal man will do; each day's intent comes wagered upon a half-hearted guess. And granting such uncertainty, where odds stand even on all sides, should not humility triumph often as judgment? In practice, no; the error falls against humility time and again.

Much risk has come with this self-serving. The less risky course must be to risk all and seek peace first.

At such insight, fear passes to elation, elation to euphoria…until something in the situation strikes his humor.

All alone, and none to entertain but him, he laughs; and the air and Earth and sky join in the joke. He yells, top of his lungs, adolescent instinct overtaking thought. Over and over until his throat is raw. The sounds are all pain and joy united, each scream the finest poetry.

By and by he comes to silence, to consider his future at length. He knows not which direction today will lead. Will he follow the girl any further, in light of this final rejection? The question seems a trifle in the brightness of this moment; he cannot imagine what compelled him so fiercely toward her. These last days ring as foolishness.

Will he set off in a new direction, then, or simply return home with apologies? While a long journey is less appealing now than a few hours ago, a beating from an old rival is in store if he stays.

He decides there is no hurry in these decisions, not with a fine spring moon celebrating just outside the door. Perhaps the dawn's first light—coming soon by his reckoning—will contain the answer he seeks.

And so he rises, called by sounds of the world, the drips of water, their little footsteps' splatters outside.

He swings the door wide and blunders into the night, straight into the deadly sharp of Matthew's blade.

L'adorsity

The one who shrugs is bridling Jonathan's mare, turns at the strange sound. They have been present for some fifteen minutes, he and Matthew, quietly amused at the yelling coming from within the hands' quarters. "Strange fellow, that L'adorsity," they have both agreed.

Now the older man is frozen with dismay at what he sees. "Matthew! What have you done?"

Matthew turns, blade in his right hand, blood on both. "He lives..."

"Not long, from the look of him." Shrugger sighs. "Check the room."

Matthew rummages through the small quarters quickly and returns, already having pocketed the two-hundred dollars he found in the pack. "The whore is not there," he reports.

The other shrugs, for a girl is an easily-replaceable

commodity, unlike the mare which holds great sentimental value to Jonathan. And now this—poor Jonathan's brother turned murderer! "Come," he says. "Drag him to the field, for he is your weight now. I will look for shovels."

Matthew wraps a weak fist 'round L'adorsity's shirt collar and begins dragging his limp form toward the wide easy meadow, making difficult progress. Shrugger returns with two shovels balanced wobbly in one hand, grabs the collar with his other hand, and helps with the load. He looks down at Skeeter, passive, mortally wounded as he is.

A trail of blood marks their going, seeping slowly into the damp earth.

"Look at you now," he tells the stricken one. "Look at you now. Thanks to your rudeness..." He glares at Matthew. "And thanks to this one's sudden appetite for blood, I am obliged to dig a grave...by sweat of my brow and callus of my hand at this tender hour of the morning..."

Matthew glares back. "Jonathan said we were to find and kill him."

"Words of temper, nothing more. To kill requires a stronger rationale than anger—a large sum of money, perhaps. Jonathan wants merely the horse returned safely; never would he approve of this act of yours. Think you we shall search all night, every one of us, over a trifle such as vengeance?"

"'twas necessary," Matthew counters. He motions at L'adorsity. "This one, always an ache in my brother's side. I was but a child and I remember their quarrels. For so long it continued, such meaningless feud. Now it is finished, and it is good."

"I knew him only for a day but, true; he seemed a pest for no good reason."

"Jonathan will thank me; this is certain."

"No." The one who shrugs takes firm tone of command,

for he is Jonathan's lieutenant. "No such thing shall be. Instead, we shall bury him here, for all believe he has fled the township forever. He will not go missing, and not a one will suspect what has occurred. Accept you this, Matthew…after we finish here, you and I never will speak of these events."

Matthew takes a look of disappointment. "Jonathan would thank me," he affirms.

"You think to honor him, make him proud?" The other softens. "You come of age today in such a fearsome way. To join our savage breed, perhaps ought not inspire delight, but resignation. A proud flavor of shame we hold within us."

They reach a soft spot in the field and begin digging.

Skeeter lies watching, too faint to speak. The surreal glow of night is like the clearest fog, the cold damp of the grass like loving hands of warmth.

Nature comes to take him at some point in the digging. In one perfect instant of nothing and everything one—a calm exhale, aware and behold! The night soaks straight through and is still.

At that last second he laments nothing—certainly not the fact that he will have no funeral. There is no soul alive who understands him sufficient to deliver a fair eulogy, save one—and her fear of him, by coincidence, carried her just in time from harm's way. He dies indeed solely that she be free of Jonathan.

His last thoughts, therefore, are for the girl who saved his life, who gave all in resistance of him, who pushed him over the edge of healing that never would he have crossed. She succeeded where the kind elder failed—being, by chance, exactly what he needed.

Nothing is for regret; to die alive is a good death, to die lifeless but a minor adjustment.

Somewhere that pure feminine soul rides unbounded, blissfully unaware of his passing. Only his essence remains etched upon her memory's window, his last loving words a kinder spirit for her travels. She rides with the rising sun at her left, hopefully to find the setting sun leading her west, to new lands and startling freedoms.

If not, no matter. Even should she take to the next township and resume her current way of life, the armor is breached sufficient by these gentle blows. Hope will assail and overcome, to fullness wherever she remains.

All is as it belongs.

The red-haired brother and the one who shrugs finish their unfortunate task, tired, but with the good feeling that hard work leaves in one's body.

"A few words, perhaps?" the larger suggests, staring passively at the grave.

Matthew snorts an unkind refusal.

Therefore Shrugger calls up some spark of overheard wisdom, and does recite these words...

Cares not the world for ideas bright
Count insight but weightless
All truth inept
'neath pond'rous weight of violence

Thus inspired, Matthew finds a flattened, withered daisy lying on the grass, perhaps where it fell from clumsy Orson's hat a few days earlier. A cackle sounds from remorseless lips, and the brave soldier is tossed upon the grave.

They mount their horses and ride, leading Jonathan's prize mare between them, back to loveless bondage.

And in the blessed meadow, crackling with the energy of life, a bare spot of earth lies freshly turned, the mark of all a man ever shall attain. In time the mark will be obscured, fresh grass grown up from its sustenance; and nature will accept the man to

DS Swanson

herself, one to all, energy of dust breathed real by momentary consciousness.

Made in the USA
San Bernardino, CA
14 May 2018